The Winning Stroke

The Winning Stroke

by Matt Christopher

Illustrated by Karin Lidbeck

 Little, Brown and Company
Boston   New York   Toronto   London

First Paperback Edition

The characters and events portrayed in this book are fictitious. Any sim-
ilarity to real persons, living or dead, is coincidental and not intended by the
author.

Library of Congress Cataloging-in-Publication Data
Christopher, Matt.
    The winning stroke / by Matt Christopher.
        p.   cm.
    Summary: When hydrotherapy for an injured leg takes him to the pool
on a regular basis, twelve-year-old Jerry finds himself fascinated and
challenged by the rigors of competitive swimming.
    ISBN: 0-316-14266-2 (hc)
    ISBN: 0-316-14128-3 (pb)

    [1. Swimming — Fiction.]   I. Title.
    PZ7.C458Wi   1994   93-40257
    [Fic] — dc20
                              MV-NY

                    10 9 8 7 6 5 4 3 2 1

Published simultaneously in Canada
by Little, Brown & Company (Canada) Limited

Printed in the United States of America

To Richard and Kathleen

The Winning Stroke

1

"Come on, Billy, come on, big guy," came a voice from behind.

As Jerry Grayson adjusted his grip on the bat, he could hear the catcher calling out encouragement to the mound.

But Billy Wolfson, the pitcher, was taking his time.

With a count of three and 0, he knows I can afford to swing at anything that looks halfway decent, thought Jerry. Too bad, Billy, but even with a two-run lead, you'd better not take any chances. After all, I'm already two for three this game.

Jerry knew that his teammates were hoping he would get on base. It was the bottom of the ninth. They had two outs, and there was no one on base. The next pitch could save the game and start a winning rally.

Billy stretched both arms behind him as he started to wind up for the pitch. He glared at Jerry, then let the ball fly.

The pitch looked as though it would be a little high and outside. But as the ball sizzled forward toward the plate, it began to curve inward.

That's just how I like 'em, Jerry thought. He drew back for an instant, then swung.

Crack!

It was a clean hit over the shortstop's head.

Jerry took off like a shot. He made it easily to first base before the left fielder had grabbed hold of the ball.

"Hold, Jerry! Hold!" shouted his teammates.

Why should I hold? Jerry thought. I'm one of the fastest runners on the team. I can stretch that hit to a double, no problem!

But Nick Dodson, the left fielder, was faster on the draw than Jerry realized. The ball was in the air and on its way to second in a flash. Jerry had to slide — or else he'd be tagged out.

A cloud of dust rose from his sneakers as he skidded toward the base.

Standing like a mountain of humanity on second base was Harry "Hulk" Harrison. Hulk was never much of a threat at bat or on the field, but his size could be intimidating. His huge body blocked the sun as he reached for the incoming ball. When it made contact with his mitt, he wheeled to tag Jerry. But his foot caught on the base and, off balance, he fell.

At any second, Jerry had expected to feel contact between the base and the sole of his sneaker. He had stretched his right leg as far as it would reach in the direction of the base.

Instead, he felt a sharp pain shooting up and down his leg as a wall of weight came crashing down on it. Hulk Harrison had tagged him out by landing on him full force.

As the dust cleared, Hulk rolled off him into the dirt. The big second baseman got up and shook off his large form. Raising his left arm, he brandished the ball still trapped in his mitt.

"Out!" Hulk shouted. "I gotcha! You're out, Jerry! We win!"

Oh, yeah? thought Jerry, all set to argue. "No way!" he shouted from down on the ground.

Suddenly, the pain in his right leg shot through his entire right side.

But he had to get up. He had to out-shout Hulk and prove he had gotten to second base safely. He leaned on one elbow and tried to raise his body from the ground. He was okay as long as the weight was on his left knee. Then he tried to move his right leg. The pain exploded, and a screaming white light filled his body before everything turned black.

Jerry woke with a start when an awful ammonia smell hit his nostrils. He opened his eyes and saw an emergency medical technician leaning over him, a concerned look in his eye.

Terrible as the smell was, it cleared his head. He was wide awake when the stretcher was carefully placed underneath him and he was carried into the waiting ambulance. Still, he could feel every jolt during the ride through downtown Bolton to the hospital.

His mother was waiting outside the Emergency Room. Inside, it seemed as if a hundred different people looked at him, poked around, and asked the same stupid questions over and over. And all the while his leg throbbed with pain.

He was just about to shout out loud that he was in agony, when a nurse came in and gave him an injection in his arm.

It took a few minutes, but the pain in his leg faded away gradually. He was feeling better when they wheeled him into another examination room.

Dr. Gold, who looked as though she might be the same age as his mom, was staring at some X-rays of his leg.

"Hmmm, pretty nice break you have there," she said.

"Aw, come on, it can't be broken," he said. "Is it really?"

"To be specific, you have a mid-shaft fracture of the tibia and the fibula," said the doctor. She pointed to a spot between his knee and ankle.

"Wow, sounds pretty bad," he said.

"It's not good," she went on. "What happened? You crash into a brick wall?"

"No," said Jerry. "It came crashing down on me." He told her about the accident.

"So it's a sports injury, my specialty," she said, moving over to the examination table. She lifted the light bandaging that covered most of his leg. Since he was flat on his back, he couldn't see what it looked like.

"What do you think?" asked Jerry. "Can you fix it pretty fast?"

"We should be able to do something," said Dr. Gold.

Jerry breathed a deep sigh of relief.

"Let's see now," she said, "how old are you?"

"Twelve," he replied.

"Hmmm, and about five feet seven, one hundred and twenty pounds," she went on. "Do you smoke?"

"Never!"

"Drink lots of milk?"

"Gallons!"

"Do your homework on time?"

Jerry hesitated. "Usually," he said.

Dr. Gold laughed. "I think we'll be able to put you back together, then."

"Great!" said Jerry. "We still have a few more games left, and the team really needs me."

"The team?" said Dr. Gold.

"Our sandlot baseball team," said Jerry. "I'm the number one hitter."

"That's nice," said Dr. Gold. "But I can't see you playing baseball for a while."

"Why not?" asked Jerry.

"Because you're going to be in a cast and have to use crutches for about eight weeks."

"What? No way!"

"Okay," said the doctor. "Then just hop off that table and get out of here."

Even with the soothing effect of the shot, Jerry knew that he couldn't move his bad leg. The slightest touch still sent shivers of pain all along the right side of his body.

"Eight weeks," he moaned. "I might as well jump off a cliff."

"That's another option," said the doctor. "Or, we can go ahead with the cast."

Jerry sighed. "But after eight weeks I'll be okay?" he asked. "I'll be able to play baseball? It'll be a little early for the school team. Maybe I'll play basketball. Still, if the ground isn't frozen —"

"Not so fast," said the doctor. "When you get out of the long cast, we'll put you into a shorter one."

"Another cast! Why don't I just crawl into bed and stay there forever!"

"Oh, the short cast is a lot easier. You'll be able to walk around on it without the crutches."

"Sure, but I bet I'm not going to be shooting hoops in it — or shagging ground balls. How long will I have to wear the darn thing?" Jerry asked.

"I'd say, about four weeks."

"And then I'll be able to play sports again?"

"Maybe," said Dr. Gold.

"Maybe!"

"Look, young man, we're not magicians," said the doctor. "I don't have a crystal ball that's going to tell me exactly how well you're going to heal. Once we take the second cast off, there'll still be a lot of work to do."

"Okay, okay," said Jerry. "Do anything you have to. Just let me know when I can play ball again."

"I didn't say *we* were going to do the work," the doctor said. "It's going to be up to you."

"Me?"

She nodded her head.

"You."

2 ≈≈≈≈≈

Three months and two weeks after the day he broke his leg, Jerry sat in a whirlpool in the local rehabilitation center. The most recent X-rays showed that the bones had set, but after the short cast had come off, Doctor Gold had ordered a program of physical therapy.

Jerry, anxious to be back on the baseball field practicing with his buddies, had told her he didn't need the therapy.

"You don't think so?" she'd asked. "Just take a good look at that leg."

With the cast off, Jerry could see what had been covered up for twelve weeks. His leg looked terrible. Compared to the normal color of his left leg, the skin on his right was all white and scruffy. Thin blue veins showed through. And Jerry could tell without even

12

flexing that the muscles were weak from lack of exercise.

"Now, here's what you're going to do," Doc Gold had said. "First of all, you're going to use this." She handed him a cane. "And second, you're going to report to Bob Fulton at this address, three times a week for two hours, for physical therapy."

Jerry stared at the cane and the slip of paper she held out. He was ready to explode with frustration. Three days a week for two hours? So much for batting practice!

But then his eye fell on his leg. All right, he figured, I'll go along with what she says. But *I'll* decide how much of this therapy I need to do to get back to full strength.

So, three days a week, right after school, Jerry reported to Bob Fulton at the rehab center. At first, he just tried to breeze through his exercises. But soon, he realized that Mr. Fulton didn't stand for any goofing off. He was giving his all — and expected nothing less from his patients. Jerry respected his straightforward manner and, even more important, he felt Mr. Fulton really cared if his leg improved.

❁   ❁   ❁

Even so, after two weeks of the same routine of exercises, Jerry was getting bored. Relaxing in the whirlpool was nice, but he itched to be doing something more strenuous than leg lifts. He missed the action of the baseball field and the friendly joking of his teammates.

So today, after he finished his session of exercises, he confessed his frustration to Bob Fulton. His therapist looked thoughtful.

"Well, I can't let you back on the baseball field quite yet, because your leg wouldn't stand the pounding of running on hard turf. But I have been considering some optional therapy for you. There's still a little stiffness around your knee and ankle, and those leg muscles need more of a workout than you're getting here. So, starting Monday, you'll be meeting me at the swimming pool at Bolton Middle School. You can swim, can't you?"

"Oh, sure," said Jerry. "I learned at the Y when I was a little kid. Gee, I never thought of swimming as therapy. I figured it's just something you do at the Y or at the beach."

"Believe me, there's a lot more to swimming than just clowning around in the water," said Mr. Fulton.

"I ought to know. I've been coaching for fourteen years."

Jerry felt a little foolish. He hadn't meant to knock the sport of swimming. He really had never thought much about it.

"Well, uh, then I guess I'll see you at the pool," said Jerry. "When do I start? And what am I supposed to do?"

"You start next Monday," said Mr. Fulton. "Come down to the pool and see me as soon as school lets out. I'll put you through your first round of exercises, and then you'll be on your own."

"See you at the pool, then," said Jerry.

That evening, after his eight-year-old brother, David, and four-year-old sister, Lucie, had gone to bed, Jerry told his parents about the doctor's and therapist's newest plan.

"I mean, swimming!" he said, grunting. "Why couldn't it be something like . . . like . . . like hockey!"

"Oh, sure, skating around on nice slippery ice," said his mother, putting down her newspaper. "That's just what you need to build up your leg."

"Right," said his father. "When your leg buckled under, the other team could skate right over you. And then you'd end up in a full body cast."

"Probably for a year," said his mother.

"At least one," said his father. "Maybe two years. Could I have the business section, Liz? I want to check out my investments in plaster of paris."

"All right, all right," Jerry grumbled. "I'll do the swimming."

When he arrived at the school pool Monday, Jerry felt uncomfortable. He was used to knowing his way around sports arenas. The baseball diamond was like a second home to him. But the pool was like a foreign country. None of the guys he knew went out for swimming as a sport. He'd just have to play it really cool and get this pool stuff over as quickly as possible.

Mr. Fulton stood in the shallow end of the school swimming pool. Jerry splashed awkwardly down the ladder beside him. The cool water raised goose bumps on his arms.

"The purpose of these exercises is to adjust your leg to different forms of stress gradually," Mr. Fulton explained.

He showed Jerry each exercise. Then he waited to make sure Jerry had them right.

At the end of the last one, Jerry clung to the edge of the pool with his fingertips while his body floated behind him just below the water.

"Now," Mr. Fulton went on, "do you have all the counts?"

"I think so," said Jerry. "I do fifty of these —" he demonstrated a kick under water. "Then I do fifty pushing with the other leg, the good one."

"Right," said Mr. Fulton. "And then?"

Jerry went down the complete list of pool exercises, which ended up with swimming a half dozen laps up and down the pool.

"How long is all this going to take?" he asked.

"About a half, maybe three-quarters of an hour," said Mr. Fulton. "That should get you out of here before swimming practice begins. Even if some of the kids get here early and do a few extra laps, you won't be in the way."

"Oh, great," Jerry mumbled.

"What's that?" asked Mr. Fulton.

"Nothing," said Jerry. "Just thinking out loud."

"Never mind thinking," said the coach. "Start

those exercises." He hoisted himself out of the pool and slipped into a pair of white rubber thongs. Toweling off, he pulled a gray Bolton sweatshirt over his head and left the pool area for his office next to the locker room.

As soon as he was gone, Jerry let go and floated out toward the middle of the pool. Now that his body was used to the temperature, the water felt good.

But not as good as sweating in the hot sun on a baseball diamond. Darn this leg, Jerry thought angrily. More exercises! And I still might not be ready for baseball season.

Suddenly, a voice broke through his thoughts. "You'll never get that leg strong enough to do anything if you don't start doing your workout." It was as if Bob Fulton had read his mind. Jerry hadn't heard him return to the pool area. He hastily paddled back to the edge of the pool and went to work.

"Forty-five, forty-six, forty-seven, forty-eight —"

Jerry counted out loud, his voice echoing through the silence of the pool area. But before he had finished, excited calls and loud splashes told him he was no longer alone.

"Hey, Fred, wanna see my new butterfly kick?"

"How'd you do in the hundred yard?"

"Don't forget to lift your head, Sally."

Just what I need, Jerry thought. A bunch of real swimmers watching me paddle back and forth. Well, the heck with them. I'm only here for therapy, anyhow.

Still, he hesitated to start his laps. Their strokes looked so smooth.

"Hi, Jerry," came a voice nearby.

It was Tanya Holman. They had known each other since kindergarten and were in the same class at school. Tanya had tucked her short, honey-blonde hair under a bathing cap. She had on a blue-and-white diagonally striped bathing suit. The others on the swimming team were wearing similar suits. Jerry had on his usual aloha print boxer-type swimming trunks. There was no mistaking him for a member of that team.

"Hi, yourself," he said. "I didn't know you swam — I mean, on the team."

"I haven't really made the first team yet," she said. "But I'm trying. I baby-sat at the beach club last summer and practiced in their pool after work."

"But hasn't the season started?" he asked.

"Uh huh. We've already won two meets — and lost two," she said. "But sometimes people drop off for one reason or another. And Coach Fulton always knows who's ready to come in as a replacement."

With that, she dived into the green depths and began her laps.

Anxious to get out of there, he got down to the same business himself. In his usual seaside fashion, he swam back and forth, paying no attention to anyone or anything. He did a nice, easy crawl that sliced neatly through the water. When he finished, he pulled himself up to the edge of the pool. To his surprise, he felt tired all over, and his leg ached. He sat for a moment to rest. Tanya swam up to him.

"Pretty good for a first baseman," she said cheerfully. He liked the way the freckles around her turned-up nose seemed to dance when she smiled.

Jerry shrugged. "I just hope I'll be back playing ball in a little while," he said. "I'm only here to make the doctor happy. She thinks I need a little more therapy. You know, for my leg."

"Right, I remember when you had the accident," she said. "But this is a pretty nice place to be if you can't play ball. Ever seen a race?"

"Sure," he said.

"In person?" Tanya asked. "You know, not on TV like the Olympics."

Jerry hesitated. "Not really," he admitted.

"Well, then, why don't you stick around for a little while and watch a few," she suggested. "Lars Morrison is going against Wayne Cabot in the hundred-yard breaststroke. They were the top two swimmers in that stroke last year, but they kept trading places for the number one spot. Coach Fulton wants to see who's the stronger this year."

As she spoke, Jerry could see two swimmers vigorously ploughing their way through the water at opposite sides of the pool.

"It'll only take a few minutes," she said.

Jerry hesitated. "I don't know, I feel kind of dumb sitting around in a wet bathing suit." He hated to admit that all he could think about right now was getting home to a hot shower and a comfortable chair to relax in.

Tanya shook her head. "Maybe some other time, then." She turned and took off like a shot, doing more laps.

Jerry sat for a minute longer, then slowly stood up.

He limped to the locker room to collect his things. He'd just pulled on his sweatshirt when he realized he'd left his towel in the bleachers.

Jerry was amazed at the change of atmosphere in the pool area. Before, all the swimmers had been in the pool, doing leisurely warm-up laps and joking around with one another. Now, only six swimmers, one per lane, were in the water. Each was swimming the crawl as if his life depended on it. The pool water sloshed over the sides from the waves they made as they raced from one end of their lanes to the other.

Shouts of encouragement rang off the tiles. Jerry heard Bob Fulton's voice boom out over the others. But he was too busy watching the lead swimmer to hear what the coach had said.

The front-runner was one arm's length away from the lane's end. Jerry expected him to slow down and turn in the water. But instead, in a movement too quick for Jerry to see clearly, the swimmer's hand brushed the pool wall and his head disappeared beneath the water. His feet broke through the surface for a split second. Then, suddenly, his head reappeared five feet from the wall — pointed in the opposite direction.

One after another, the other swimmers performed the same swift turn. Jerry's eye was too slow to figure out how they reversed direction. It seemed they were doing a somersault of some sort.

What a crazy sport, Jerry thought. Then the race came to an end, the lead swimmer winning easily.

He could see Coach Fulton talking to the guys who would be racing next. Since they were all wearing the same practice suits, they looked an awful lot alike. But gradually he could see differences. Lars Morrison, with deep auburn hair, had wide shoulders and long skinny arms. Wayne Cabot, with wavy brown hair, was a few inches shorter but much more muscular. He looked as if he might be a weight lifter when he wasn't swimming.

Suddenly, the group around the coach broke up. One by one the swimmers took their places on the blocks at the edge of the pool. Jerry realized another race was about to start and quickly took a seat in the bleachers.

Everyone had quieted down now. All eyes were focused on the lineup of swimmers in blue-and-white striped suits poised and ready to plunge forward.

As he saw them crouch slightly to get the most spring, the athlete in Jerry began to stir. He, too, could sense the tension. He, too, could feel the cold, clammy chill of excitement surrounding the pool.

Screeeeeeech!

The whistle blew, and the swimmers were off like a shot.

3 〜〜〜〜〜

The six swimmers worked their way up and down the pool, arms drawing the water back as their legs flashed beneath the surface. Jerry had a little trouble seeing who was ahead. Wayne and Lars, swimming in lanes next to one another, were at least three feet ahead of the others.

At first, it looked as if Wayne had the lead. His muscular arms worked furiously, his shoulders knotted with exertion, dragging his body forward by their sheer power. But, then, Lars slipped ahead. His long arms parted the water in front of him in clean, regular strokes.

As they started the fourth and final lap, they were side by side, so close it was impossible for Jerry to see who was ahead. It really didn't matter. He just wanted one of them, clearly the two best swimmers in the pool, to be the winner.

"Come on, Lars! Come on, Wayne!"

He found himself shouting and cheering along with the other spectator swimmers.

People must think I'm nuts, he figured. I don't care. I just want to see the best one win!

And then it was over. In a final burst of speed, someone had touched the edge of the pool first. Coach Bob Fulton had been crouched right there in his white thongs, watching to see whose extended fingertip had made first contact with the tile.

Now, the coach stood up and blew his whistle for attention.

"The winner is — Lars Morrison!" he announced.

There was a scattering of applause from the stands. Lars and Wayne slapped high fives on each other. Then they splashed a little water in fun at the other guys and climbed out of the pool.

"So, what did you think?" asked Tanya.

Jerry had been so caught up in the race, he hadn't seen her come up beside him. She stood next to him carrying a jacket and an armful of books.

"It was okay," he admitted. "Is that it? I mean, are there any more races?"

"No, we had a meet last Saturday, so Coach made it a light workout for the team today," she said. "Some of the others will do some extra laps now, but I have a lot of homework. Are you ready to leave?" she asked.

"Sure," he said.

As they left the pool area, he glanced back and saw Lars and Wayne. Both of them were thrashing their way through the water again. You couldn't even tell that they'd been in a race a few minutes ago. They really must love swimming, he thought. I don't get it.

Dr. Gold and Coach Fulton had agreed that Jerry should do his pool therapy only every other day. So he wasn't back in the pool until Wednesday after school.

As he got into his swimming trunks, he felt a little more at home than he had on Monday. He wondered whether there would be a regular team practice today. Who would be there? Both the guys and the girls? Would Tanya be swimming again?

Would Lars? Wayne? And what was practice like, anyhow?

With those thoughts running through his head, he got into the water to begin his therapy. Therapy? Hah! It was a real workout. He was surprised to find his arms still hurt from Monday's laps. It sure was nothing like the warm-up exercises he'd done at baseball practice last year. Gee, they'd probably be getting set for spring training, and he'd be splashing around in a stinky old swimming pool.

"Forty-eight, forty-nine, fifty! Done!"

He'd finished the last exercise. The pool was still empty. None of the members of the swim team had arrived for their practice yet. He was all alone in this big space, surrounded by the tiled walls, the wooden seats, the sunken lights, and the cool, green water. All he had left was his swimming laps.

As he swam up and down the pool in his usual lazy crawl, his arm muscles started to loosen up. His leg still hurt a bit, but it wasn't as bad as Monday. By the time he'd done four laps, he was feeling much better. And he was no longer alone. Several others were parting the waves in different lanes.

As Jerry pulled himself out of the water, he wondered if these swimmers felt like part of a team. Sure, they had uniforms and a great coach, but it wasn't the same thing as running out on the field with eight other guys at the start of the game. And warm-ups in baseball meant throwing the ball around with your teammates, not plowing through the water in your own lane. You won a game because your team worked like a well-oiled machine, each player doing his part. In swimming, the team members competed against one another!

Still, as Jerry toweled off, he could feel a kind of team spirit float over the water.

Yeah, but it's weird, Jerry thought. Why would anyone choose this sport over baseball or another team sport?

That got him thinking about baseball tryouts. They'd be starting any day now. He might not be able to join the team right away. But even Doc Gold had said he should be able to play later in the season. Maybe he could pinch-hit or fill in if someone got sick.

Jerry tried to push the image of himself sitting on

the bench as far from his mind as possible. It was too painful to imagine waiting in vain for someone on the team to drop out.

"Hey, you're becoming a regular swimming fan!" The voice at his elbow startled him out of his gloomy thoughts.

"Well, I can't really play baseball yet," he said. "It helps pass time."

"You ought to think about swimming," said Tanya. "I saw you doing your laps. You're not all that bad."

"Laps? Oh, you mean my therapy."

"Whatever you call it, I've seen worse," she said.

"Yeah, well, I'll stick to my exercises," he said. "That's what's going to get my leg back in shape so I can play baseball."

But that Friday, after he had whipped through his routine exercises, he found himself looking forward to swimming his laps.

Coach Fulton came by and watched him do the first two runs back and forth. "Let's put a little more zip into it," he called. "Get that blood circulating!"

Jerry tried to swim harder, but he didn't manage to go any faster.

When he climbed out of the pool, the coach was

gone. He knew that there was another half hour before practice because he had checked the schedule outside the coach's office. As usual, a few early birds had arrived and started their warm-up on the other side of the pool. Tanya was one of them. She left a group of girls and came over to talk to him.

"Not bad," she said. "Until the coach yelled at you and you choked."

Despite the coolness of the water, Jerry's face burned.

"I didn't choke," he protested.

"Yes, you did," she said matter-of-factly. "You tried too hard and you got sloppy. I do it all the time. Everyone does. But I'm getting better."

"I can see," he said.

"You know what would really help me?"

"What?" he asked.

"If someone would swim with me when I do my extra practice," she said. "I hate doing it alone. It feels strange being all by myself in the pool — not like competition. What do you think? Would you mind helping me out?"

"Me? Swim with you?"

"I'm not asking you to jump blindfolded off the

high diving board," she said. She took off her bathing cap and shook out her short blonde hair. "I'll just come by at the end of your therapy. We can do laps side by side, okay?"

"Well, okay, I guess so," he said. "My exercises are getting real boring. Maybe doing the laps with someone will make my leg heal quicker."

"Uh huh," she said. "Just one more thing."

"What's that?"

"Get a decent swimsuit," she said, giggling.

4

On Monday, Tanya showed up at the pool just as Jerry finished his last leg exercise. Without a word, she jumped into the pool and got ready to start her laps.

"Okay, six laps?" said Jerry, wiping off his face with his palm. She nodded, and he moved into a lane right next to her.

"Ready, set, go!" she shouted. And off they went.

Jerry kept up with her at first. But to his surprise and embarrassment, he finished almost a full lap behind. And then, as he cooled off and stood there in the water, she swam two more laps before quitting.

Beaten by a *girl!* Jerry groaned inwardly. Get me out of this pool and onto the baseball diamond! Then he heard a familiar footstep behind him.

"Nice stroke, Tanya," said the coach. He paused

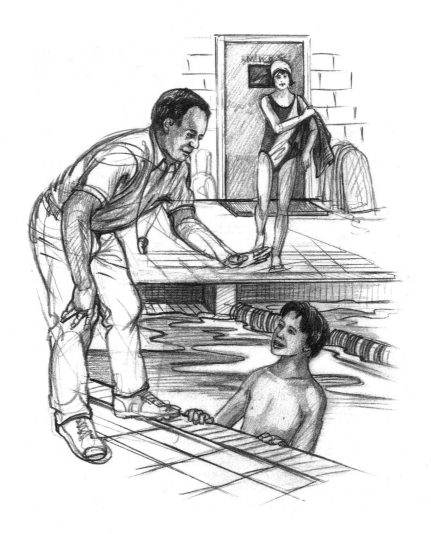

and looked at Jerry. For a minute, Jerry thought he was going to say something about *his* stroke. Instead, he just asked, "How do you like swimming against someone?"

"It's okay, I guess," Jerry replied. But I'd like it much better if I won, he added silently.

The coach went on. "Why don't you come to practice some time next week and work out against some of the guys? Not that Tanya can't give you some real competition. But mixing it up might be a good change. We only do an hour workout on Mondays, and I think it would benefit your leg. It certainly won't hurt it."

"Well, okay, if you think it'll help," said Jerry. But secretly, he wasn't sure he'd like it all that much. Losing to Tanya was bad enough — now the whole team would see him come in last!

"I'm sure it'll be good for you," said the coach. "You can cut the exercises in half. And skip the laps. You'll get enough of those in practice."

Tanya was patting herself down with a towel when Jerry came out of the pool.

"I overheard what the coach said. Don't worry — he wouldn't suggest you swim with the team if he didn't think you could keep up. And by the way, nice threads," she said, admiring his new navy blue swimmer's briefs.

He smiled. Secretly, he was glad his mother had gotten them for him at the mall on Saturday. It really did feel a lot better cutting through the water than when he had his aloha trunks on. And, after all, since they were dark, he figured no one would notice him when he showed up at practice.

Over the weekend, Jerry tried not to think about what it would be like at the pool with all those kids who were really into swimming. He was used to being in top shape for any sport he played. Even though baseball was his number one choice, he liked to play touch football, too. He was a terrific passer, and he loved scoring touchdowns. He also loved playing one-on-one basketball with his kid brother in front of the garage and could hold his own with any of the kids on the street. But swimming, real sports swimming, was something new. He decided he'd just be cool and push it out of his mind until the time came.

Instead, he spent his time doing a few chores he'd

put off for a while. He started out by giving the family dog, Yogi, a good brushing. The gray-and-white miniature schnauzer loved to be brushed, and Jerry really put some effort into it.

"Don't wear out that brush," his father called over to him as he vacuumed the inside of his car.

The two of them were alone in the garage, doing their respective jobs.

"I've gotten so used to counting," said Jerry. "I gave her fifty strokes on one side, then fifty on another, then fifty on her back . . . and then I lost count and started all over again! Say, Dad, what do you think of swimming?"

"A little early for a trip to the beach, I'd say," replied Mr. Grayson.

"I mean competitive swimming, as a sport," Jerry said.

"I think it's great," said his father. "Takes a lot of discipline as well as ability. You can get a lot of satisfaction out of swimming for a long time, even after you stop competing. Why? Are you thinking of taking it up?"

"Nah," said Jerry. But in the back of his mind, he was thinking about what Tanya had said. Did Coach

Fulton really think he could hold his own against the more seasoned swimmers?

By Monday afternoon, Jerry could hardly wait for classes to end. You might think I was going to batting practice, he said to himself. But, instead, the minute the closing bell rang, he made his way over to the poolside locker room. He changed into his new blue nylon swimsuit and headed for the pool.

There was still a half hour before team practice began, plenty of time to do his exercises.

"Twenty-four, twenty-five!"

He looked up at the clock. Ten minutes to go.

The pool quickly began to fill up with boys and girls. He now recognized one or two from classes.

Tanya came in talking to Tony Kendrix, who was in his earth science class. Tony was almost a foot taller than Tanya, but he was all legs. He had jet-black curly hair that looked like a mop on his head from the other side of the pool. But he was no one to laugh at. When he dropped the towel that was draped around his shoulders, Jerry could see how muscular his upper body was, like a weight lifter's.

Tanya and Tony joined the others in the pool,

paddling about, showing each other certain moves, and generally having a good time.

Coach Fulton interrupted their playing around by blowing his whistle. Before he even said a word, the boys and girls started separating. Jerry automatically fell in with the boys over on his side of the pool.

"Okay, I want three lanes each," he said. "We have a one-hour practice today, and I want to spend it on the backstroke. Everybody swims. But for now, let's just have three swimmers to a lane, the first one in each lane in the pool. The rest of you, come on out."

Jerry's heart pounded. Now that he was actually taking part in a practice, he realized how little he knew about how they were run. He was grateful that he was number five in his lane. This way he'd get to see how the drill worked before he had to do anything. He'd also get to watch how others did the backstroke, a stroke he was only a little familiar with.

With these thoughts racing through his mind, he found a spot near the edge of the pool that would give him a good view of the drill.

Standing in the shallow end of the pool, the line of boys and girls turned their backs to the pool. Each gripped the legs of a diving podium and, with their knees bent and their feet flat against the wall, they pulled themselves into a crouching position. When Coach Fulton blew the whistle, they let go of the bars and pushed off from the pool wall as hard as they could. Once the first line of six swimmers had begun their laps, the second line got into position and waited for the whistle. The water churned as six, then twelve, then eighteen swimmers filled the lanes.

The coach and his assistants walked along one long side of the pool, across the deep side, then down the other, and back to the beginning, calling out instructions.

Even from where he sat, Jerry could tell that some swimmers were better than others. Some looked really clumsy and almost drifted into the neighboring lane. Not everyone was a top-notch performer.

That gave him a little boost. He had done the backstroke in his Y swimming class years ago, and once in a while at the beach, but it wasn't something he was very good at. In a few minutes, though, he'd be out there doing it under the coach's watchful gaze. He didn't want to make a fool of himself.

"Come on, Freddy, get that kick going! Sally,

stretch those arms! Nice work, Lars. Push, Wayne, push!"

The coaches kept it up for a few more minutes. Then the whistle blew.

Jerry thought that everyone would leap up and scamper out of the pool. Instead, they finished their laps and treaded water for a moment before leaving the pool. He made a mental note to remember to cool down afterward, just as with any sport or exercise.

"Okay, next group," called Coach Fulton.

Jerry got back into the lane he'd been in before. This time he was second in line. He watched very carefully as the boy in front of him stood with his back to the others and pushed off along with the kids in the other five lanes.

A few seconds elapsed, and it was Jerry's turn. He did what he thought everyone else was doing. He pushed off from the edge and began swimming hard.

He was cautious at first, but began to stroke harder after a few seconds.

"Let's get those legs kicking! Slice that water, Miller! Push, everyone, push!"

Jerry concentrated on everything he could remember about the backstroke from his early training. He barely heard the coach's shouts. But when his name was mentioned, he couldn't mistake it.

"Stay in your own lane, Grayson!"

A second later his arm crashed down on the lane divider — and on someone's head.

Jerry completely lost his stroke and floundered in the water. Luckily, it was near the end of a lap and he was able to wade out of the water before Wayne Cabot, his lane mate, ran into him. Jerry grinned sheepishly at Wayne. But Wayne merely raised an eyebrow and looked away. Jerry felt about two feet tall.

"Okay, now that everyone has done his or her own backstroke, let's take a look at the right way to do it," said Coach Fulton. "Some of you are close, but some of you have a long way to go. Everyone out of the water — except you, Lars. You're going to help me show how it's done right."

Jerry, still smarting from Wayne's snub, took his seat in the stands to watch the demonstration.

"You'll get the hang of it after a while," said a voice nearby. It was Tony Kendrix.

"Yeah, but I feel like an idiot, bumping into someone," said Jerry.

"I know," said Tony. "It was me you bumped into." He laughed good-naturedly then turned his attention toward the pool.

For the next ten minutes, the coach demonstrated the different types of kicks, how to propel the arms, the right way to curve the hand so that it sliced the water, and how to push through with the thighs.

Wow, thought Jerry. There's so much more than I remember from before. But if these guys can learn it, I'm sure I can.

"Okay, we'll split up into twos now," Coach Fulton announced. "The first six in the lanes will start off, the second six will be the coaches, the next six will be swimmers, and so on. And then we'll reverse."

Jerry watched as the first group went through their workout. He was amazed at how tough the "coaches" were on their swimmers.

"You call that a kick?"

"What are you, an airplane propeller?"

"Come on, Ellen, get those arms working!"

They made Coach Fulton and his assistants seem tame.

Wayne Cabot turned out to be Jerry's coach. He didn't stop shouting the whole time Jerry was swimming.

"Oh, boy, it's amateur hour! Hey, you're not out there to make snow angels! It's not called the flapstroke, you know!"

Jerry felt like telling him a thing or two — and climbing out of the pool once and for all. But he wasn't a quitter. He was determined to get it right. Still, the harder he tried, the worse it seemed to get. There was no way he was going to do the backstroke right.

"Nice kick, Grayson," came a voice deeper than Wayne's. Coach Fulton had been watching. He'd seen one thing Jerry was doing well and shouted encouragement. It was just what Jerry needed to keep going.

Finally, the whistle blew, and they switched off. Jerry was now Wayne's "coach." He could hardly wait to yell out his criticisms.

But the veteran swimmer seemed to be doing everything right. Jerry couldn't see a single thing to shout about.

The last group of coaches and swimmers finished their turns, and Coach Fulton signaled that practice was over. Jerry wandered off by himself toward the locker room.

He'd been amazed by how rough everyone was on each other. Everyone seemed to be trying to be the best. There was no thought of the whole team. This sure was a lot different from baseball, where you all had to play together. In baseball, you were part of a real team. In swimming, you did your own thing and that was that. Jerry wasn't sure he was cut out for a sport like that.

As he left the pool locker room, he was surprised to see some of his baseball buddies heading out to the field.

"Hey, Jerry, you're finally out of that cast. So how's it going?" called Phil Fanelli. Phil had been the best southpaw on Jerry's sandlot team and shoo-in for a spot on the school team.

"Okay, what are you guys up to?" asked Jerry.

"A little early practice," said Phil. "Shake out the kinks, you know. Kind of nice out there now. You feel like playing some ball?"

Jerry hesitated. His glove was in his gym locker, and there was no reason he couldn't play in his jeans and T-shirt. But was his leg strong enough?

Just then, Wayne Cabot entered the locker room. "Hey, Grayson," he called. "Forgot to mention it when you were paddling around out there earlier, but your push-off from the wall was weak. You need to explode into action at the start of every race, even if it's just a practice lap. Might as well start doing it the right way now." With that, he picked up his towel and headed toward the showers.

Jerry's face burned. *I'd like to get him out in the batting cage — then we'd see who was weak!*

He opened his locker, pulled out his glove, and said to Phil, "I'll meet you guys out on the diamond. I just have to shower this stupid chlorine off."

Fifteen minutes later, Jerry was poised at home plate, waiting for Phil to pitch to him. Phil reared back and threw a fastball. Jerry connected solidly and took off for first base.

Within seconds, Jerry knew he shouldn't be running. His leg screamed in pain with every step. He limped his way off the field and sank down onto the bench. He'd never felt so defeated in his life.

5 〜〜〜〜

"Uh huh. Uh huh," said Jerry. "Uh huh. Yeah. Uh huh. Right."

He was sitting on a tall stool and talking into the telephone as his mother walked through the hallway carrying a mug of hot coffee.

"Fascinating conversation," she said.

Blowing across the mug, she went into the living room and turned on the early news.

"Okay, gotta go," said Jerry. "Bye."

He hung up and went into the kitchen.

After a moment, Mrs. Grayson followed him in. He was seated at the table with a huge slice of apple pie and a tall glass of milk in front of him.

"Okay, what's on your mind?" she asked, sitting down at the table.

"What do you mean?"

"You always head for the refrigerator when there's something on your mind," she said. "And that's a pretty large snack an hour before dinner. So something must be going on up there." She patted him on the head.

"Oh, I was just talking to Tanya about baseball," he said.

"What about it? You're not ready to play ball yet, are you?" she asked, sipping on her coffee.

"Mmmm, I was . . . I mean, I thought I was . . . I mean, well . . ." He didn't quite know how to explain.

"Why don't you start from the beginning," she suggested.

So Jerry told her about what had happened that day in the pool and later, on the baseball diamond. "I'm just not used to not being able to run!" he blurted out.

"Seems to me you're not used to learning anything new when it comes to sports — any sport."

Jerry was quiet for a moment. Then he said, "I guess you're right. I'm used to just playing sports naturally."

"You're only working out with the other swimmers," said his mother. "You're not in competition with them, you know."

"Right," he said, nodding. "But I don't want to look like a nerd, even in the swimming pool. I mean, you should've seen how good some of those guys were. And some of the girls were even better."

"Well, if you really want to get to their level, there's only one way to get there," she said. "Practice."

"I know," he said. "That's what Tanya was talking about just now on the phone. She's worried that she's not going to make the girls team. That's why she gets to the pool early every afternoon. She said I could work out with her if I met her there. She'll show me some drills and give me some pointers on my stroke. But I hate it when she leaves me in her backwash. I mean, she's a lot better than me."

"So what are you going to do about it?" asked Mrs. Grayson.

Jerry sighed a deep, deep sigh. "I guess I'm going to put in the extra time when I can — and I'm going to keep my ears open and my mouth shut during practice."

Mrs. Grayson grinned. "Keeping your mouth shut is always a good idea when you're in the water!"

By the time Jerry finished his leg exercises the next afternoon, more than a dozen kids were already thrashing back and forth in the pool. Even with her cap on, he recognized Tanya in the first lane. She was practicing the breaststroke, pushing the water away in front of her with a steady motion.

When she caught his eye, she stopped, cooled down, then climbed out of the pool.

"Okay, let's get organized," she said. "First, there's a set of out-of-the-water drills you can do for each stroke. Let's start with the one you're most worried about."

"The backstroke," he said without hesitation.

"Just because you swam into Tony's lane doesn't mean you were a total mess," Tanya said, smiling at him. "Here, let me show you how to practice the basic moves while you're standing up. First of all, here's a drill to develop your kick."

She worked with him for about ten minutes, then left him to practice on his own while she returned to the pool.

Jerry noticed for the first time that there were others doing exercises outside the water. Several kids stood against walls raising arms or legs, bending, or kicking, in a repeat pattern. He could hear some of them counting out loud, but otherwise there wasn't much said.

I guess swimmers don't talk to each other a lot, he thought.

"Arch that back!" Tanya shouted from the pool.

Well, at least someone had something to say to him. At least someone was cheering him on.

As he was doing his kick drills, Tony Kendrix showed up at the pool. Tony did a few breaststroke laps, then flipped over and did an even number of backstrokes. As he slid into the water, Jerry thought, I wish it could be that easy for me.

He pushed off from the side of the pool, kicked his legs, and began to cut through the water in an easy overarm motion. His head was slightly out of the water, but he didn't notice at first that someone had begun to swim alongside him at the same pace. When he did, there was too much water spray in his way to make out who it was.

The two swimmers kept it up, back and forth, lap

after lap, until Jerry wasn't sure who was keeping up with whom. He knew that he wasn't trying to out-swim his neighbor. It was just nice to have someone working away at the same pace.

Finally, Jerry's energy began to give out. He slowed down during the final lap and almost floated the few feet to the edge of the pool where he'd begun.

His neighbor stopped, too, and Jerry saw right away who it was: Tony Kendrix.

"You know, you've got a real nice crawl there," said Tony, floating over toward Jerry.

"I wish my backstroke was as easy to do," said Jerry.

"Yeah, I saw you had some trouble there," said Tony. "Don't worry about it. Just keep practicing."

Jerry smiled.

"I mean it. You'll see. It'll get easier and easier. Just like my crawl."

"Nothing wrong with that," said Jerry. "You proba-bly could have beaten me by a mile if you turned on the steam."

"That's not what I was practicing," said Tony. "I'm trying to learn to pace myself so I don't use all my energy right away and then fade. That's why I was glad to see you doing laps, nice and easy. Like I said, you've got a pretty good handle on the crawl."

"Thanks," said Jerry.

"Feel like doing eight nice steady laps and then going for broke for two more?"

"Okay," said Jerry. "I'll give it a try."

The two boys pushed off and began to make their way down their lanes. Kicking their legs behind them, they churned up the water while keeping a steady pace. Jerry felt relaxed and comfortable as one lap turned into another. Before he knew it, they had done the first eight and it was time for the final sprint.

It was no contest. Tony finished an easy fifteen feet ahead of him.

Jerry just about made it to the edge of the pool. He was out of breath and, despite the water all around, his throat was bone dry.

"Take it easy," said Tony. "You'll be okay in a minute. Hey, you did real well. I didn't know if you'd be able to go the distance."

"Thanks," said Jerry, panting a little. He got his breath back and went on, "You know, it's funny. I didn't even have to think about it, but I stayed in my lane. How come that doesn't happen when I do the backstroke?"

"Probably 'cause you're keeping your eyes straight ahead when you do the crawl. Next time you do the backstroke, try this — find an object directly in front of you as you swim. Keep your eye on it as you're swimming. It's called 'spotting' and should help you stay centered. I usually spot on my diving podium for the first lap, then the lane number on the way back," said Tony. "But another problem could be that one leg's stronger than the other. It's pulling you to one side."

"I never thought of that," said Jerry.

"Maybe you should try a different kind of kick," Tony suggested.

"Different?" asked Jerry.

Tony flipped onto his back and held on to the side of the pool. With his feet extended and toes pointed, he kicked one leg after the other up and down. Then he got up and stood in the shallow water.

"That's the flutter. You sort of kick your legs from your hips. Most people tend to bend their knees, but that uses too much energy and doesn't really work," said Tony. "Tell you what, why don't you give it a try? I'll watch and see how you're doing. Try it holding on. Then do a couple of laps."

The pool had become a little crowded as other early swimmers filled the lanes. But Jerry didn't pay much attention to them. The lane he was using was open, so he did the exercise and then began the backstroke the way he'd just seen Tony do it.

It was amazing. After just a few strokes, he knew he was doing it better. Kicking from the hips seemed a little awkward, but he was starting to get the hang of it. And he made sure he "spotted" on the podium. It made a lot of difference.

As he made his way down his lane, he heard a couple of loud splashes as some other kids jumped into the pool. In a few seconds, he realized there were people swimming alongside him.

In the distance, he heard laughter and shouting.

"Hey, look, it's 'Willy the Whale' upside down!"

"Naw, you dummy, that's just Mark Spitz — on a bad, bad day!"

The swimmer on his side kicked up a storm and passed him, followed by another.

"Come on, Lars! Come on Wayne!"

All the commotion was too much for Jerry. He lost his concentration and started kicking from his knees. He tried to regain his stroke, but a second later he crashed headfirst into the edge of the pool.

As he stood up, he could see a race in progress next to him. Lars and Wayne were racing each other, doing the backstroke with the style of real champions.

I must have looked like a real chump alongside the two of them, Jerry thought, rubbing his head.

Lars came in first, followed by Wayne just a few seconds after him.

"You were great," shouted a girl with long jet-black hair. She ran up to him and gave him a big hug.

Another girl, with deep brown eyes and wavy brown hair rushed over to Wayne.

"You'll beat him next time," she said, putting her hand in his. "Come on, Gail, let's go. We don't want to be late for that movie."

"Okay, Jennifer," said the other girl. "See you guys tomorrow." As she left, she looked over at Jerry and started to giggle.

Jerry turned bright red. He started to stomp off

toward the locker room when Tony caught up with him.

"Relax, Jerry," said Tony. "They're just a couple of show-offs when their girlfriends are around. They don't mean anything by it."

"Some fun!" snarled Jerry.

"Whoa! You look like you could bite the head off a crocodile!" said Tony. "Maybe you ought to be in a Tarzan movie! Take it easy, Jerry. Lars and Wayne are really good guys when you get to know them."

Yeah, thought Jerry, but who says I really want to get to know anyone else on the swimming team. The team I'm interested in plays on a dirt-track diamond, surrounded by grass. I wish I was there right now.

6 〰〰〰

The next afternoon, Jerry skipped practice at the pool. The minute classes were over, he marched down the school steps, still limping a little, and went home.

He was up in his room oiling his baseball glove, when his mother called up to him.

"Jerry! Can you come down here, please?"

He carefully put the glove and the oil away in his closet, and went downstairs. A strong smell of something baking was in the air. He followed the aroma into the kitchen and found a surprise.

Tanya and Tony were seated at the kitchen table.

"We could smell your mother's chocolate chip cookies a mile away," Tony explained, with a silly grin.

Jerry said, "Yeah, sure."

Tanya gave him a look that seemed to say, "You dumbbell." At least, that's how it appeared to him.

"There's more milk in the fridge," said Mrs. Grayson. "Help yourselves. I have to pick up your father at the dentist, Jerry. I'll see you later." She put on her coat and went out the back door to the garage.

"So what are you guys doing here?" Jerry asked. He eyed a chocolate chip cookie, but he didn't pick it up.

"I told you, we're here for the cookies," said Tony. He stuffed his mouth with another one.

"Oh, cut it out," said Tanya. "We're here to talk to you about swimming practice. You skipped it today."

"So what? I don't have to go to practice, you know," said Jerry. "I'm not trying out for the team."

"What about your exercises? You know, for your leg?" asked Tanya.

"I can do them when I want," said Jerry. "How do you know I didn't do them at the Y?"

"The Y pool is used for diving practice in the afternoon," said Tony. "Can't swim there for another half hour."

"Maybe I'll go then," said Jerry.

"Aw, you're just sore 'cause Lars and Wayne

showed you up yesterday," said Tony. "That's so dumb. I told you they were just fooling around."

"Yeah, but everybody else was laughing, too," said Jerry. "Their girlfriends thought it was great the way they made me look like a chump. Boy, if it was out on the baseball diamond, I could show them a thing or two!"

"What if one of them had a real natural swing at bat? If one of them could really hit the ball once he learned a thing or two?" asked Tanya. "Wouldn't you want him to play for the team?"

"Sure, but he'd have to show he could really hit all the time, that he wasn't just a flash in the pan," said Jerry.

"And how, Mr. Sports-Expert, would you be able to tell that?" asked Tanya.

"You could tell in practice," said Jerry. "And after he played a few games."

"That does it," said Tony, getting up from the table. "If you substitute swimming for baseball, you could have been talking about yourself."

"What do you mean?" asked Jerry.

"Sit down, Tony, and let's explain a few things to him," said Tanya.

"You start," said Tony, sitting back down at the table and picking at the edge of another cookie.

"You have a terrific natural crawl, Jerry," said Tanya. "I saw it when you were doing your laps that first day at the pool. Remember how I told you that you were pretty good for a baseball player?"

"Yeah, but when we did laps together, you were better. You beat me by a mile," he said.

"Right, because I've been practicing for a long time. And, besides, I knew what I was doing in a race," she said.

"Yeah, it takes more than a natural crawl," said Tony. "How do you think people like Lars and Wayne got so good? And they didn't even have the advantage of a natural stroke to start out with. I've seen Lars practice nothing but the breaststroke or the butterfly for hours. And Wayne still puts in time doing land drills for the backstroke. So do I. So does every good swimmer."

"So you think I might be a pretty good swimmer if I worked at it?" Jerry asked.

"I'm sure you could develop a great crawl without much trouble," said Tanya. "But to be a really good swimmer, you have to know all the strokes —

butterfly, backstroke, and breaststroke, too. You have to know how to dive and how to turn. And you have to know the rules."

Jerry was surprised to hear the serious tone in Tanya's voice. Did she think he wasn't enough of an athlete to learn all that? He would show her — and Tony — and Lars and Wayne, too. But there was still something holding him back.

"What about Coach Fulton? How come he never told me I should go out for the team?" Jerry asked.

"He probably wanted you to decide for yourself," said Tony. "He doesn't like to put pressure on anyone."

"I have to admit he was pretty nice when I was doing my therapy at the rehab center," said Jerry.

"He's the same at the pool," said Tanya. "Except when he sees someone goofing off or not making an effort. Then he can be a real shark!"

"So, you think if I asked him if I could try out for the team, I mean as a replacement or something, he'd help me learn all that stuff?" asked Jerry.

"Only one way to find out," said Tony. "Hey, was that the last cookie?"

Jerry wiped the crumbs off his face and smiled.

After Tanya and Tony left, Jerry went for a walk down the street. Sometimes, if he sat too long, his leg still stiffened up a little. Walking it off made him feel better.

He found himself heading in the direction of the neighborhood playground. That was where his accident had happened on the baseball diamond so many weeks back. As he approached, he could hear voices.

"Come on, Sonny, let 'er rip!"

"Easy out, Jimmy, easy out!"

A couple of the guys he used to play ball with were fooling around with an old tennis ball and a broom handle. It wasn't like real baseball, but it still stirred up the old feelings in him.

"Hey, Sonny. Hi, Pete. How's it going, Jimmy?" he called over to them.

"Great," shouted Jimmy from the mound. "Soon as I woof this guy!"

He did. In three swings and misses, Sonny went down.

Pete got up next. He hit the ball on the second try. According to the unofficial sandlot rules, that put him on first base.

"What do you say, Jerry? Want to send him all the way home?" called Jimmy.

Jerry looked at the field. There was no one around except the three guys. And it wasn't a real baseball game. It couldn't hurt to take a few swings.

"Just a couple of swings," he said to the others. "I . . . I gotta be home in time for supper."

"Sure," said Jimmy. He flashed a big grin.

Jerry could tell he was dying to strike out the sandlot batting champ. Well, I'll give him a good workout, he thought.

He gripped the sawed-off broom handle in his old familiar way. It was so much lighter than a bat, he was a little awkward at first.

Two pitches went by. All four guys argued whether they were strikes or balls. Jerry found he could still out-shout the others, and they were declared balls.

The third pitch was straight down the middle.

"Thwunk!"

The broom handle connected, and the ball went sailing deep over the pitcher's head.

With a smile, Jerry dropped the broom handle, turned up his jacket collar, and called over, "See you later, guys. I gotta go."

Not bad, he thought, but not ready. Still not ready to play baseball. The thought turned over and over in his mind as he made his way home. But I can still play sports. Swimming is a sport, after all.

Just before the next swimming practice, Jerry went over and spoke to Coach Fulton.

"I was thinking," he said. "I was wondering if you thought it would be okay, you know, for my leg, that is. I mean, I thought I might try out for a spot on the swimming team, if you'd be willing to teach me the rules and stuff."

Coach Fulton put down his clipboard and extended his hand to Jerry.

"I think it would be terrific," he said, shaking Jerry's hand. "You have a lot of athletic ability and a nice easy crawl. It would be a shame to waste it. And I'd be happy to show you how to improve your other strokes. I can't promise you a spot right away, but you keep working at your swimming and learning all the strokes, well, I think something will turn up." He picked up his clipboard. "I'll just add your name to the roster."

From that day on, Jerry worked out every afternoon with the swim team — but still did his leg exercises beforehand. Sometimes he would swim with Tony and Tanya, sometimes he'd practice by himself. But those two became his regular pals and strongest supporters.

Tony worked with him mostly on the butterfly and the breaststroke. Jerry took to the first one pretty easily. He had a lot more trouble with the breaststroke.

"Come on," said Tony. "It's fun when you get the hang of it. Let's start off with a little land drill."

Jerry groaned. He knew what that meant: flapping his arms and legs about while he was still outside the pool. He always felt a little stupid doing land drills.

But he soon mastered a basic breaststroke and could hold his own while doing laps with Tony.

And after a little practice with Tanya, he started feeling more and more comfortable, too, with the backstroke.

But his greatest pleasure was in doing sprints with either one of them using his overhand crawl. Neither of them said much in the way of pointers. He figured he had that stroke down pretty well on his own.

At the end of two weeks' time, Jerry's head was spinning with everything he had learned about the different strokes. "Next week," Tanya said with a twinkle in her eye, "we'll start teaching you about flip turns, hand touches, medleys, false starts, disqualifications —"

"Whoa! Slow down! No more!" groaned Jerry. He held his nose and ducked under water. But not before he saw Tanya grinning at him.

He came up for air just as Coach Fulton blew his whistle. "Okay, everybody, listen up," he said. "You all know we've got a meet tomorrow, ten A.M. sharp. Even if you're not scheduled to swim, I'd like you to be here, in uniform, to cheer your teammates on. Remember, all your names will be on the roster in case I have to bring you in as a substitute for any reason. But for now, everyone hit the showers, and get a good night's sleep!"

7

The day of the meet, Jerry was more excited than he ever imagined. He could barely drink his orange juice, and his vitamin pill felt like the Rock of Gibraltar on its way down his throat.

"How about a nice big bowl of oatmeal?" his mother asked.

Jerry just shook his head and ran upstairs to make sure his gym bag was packed. It felt so funny with nothing much more than a bathing suit in it. This sure was different from baseball. He glanced into his closet. There was his glove, all oiled and ready for use. That's okay, he thought, still time for baseball as soon as the leg is one hundred percent.

Mr. Grayson had another session scheduled at the dentist, so his mother drove him to the pool for the meet.

"Are you sure you don't want me to come?" she asked. "Your Aunt Helen said she wouldn't mind driving your father home from the dentist if he doesn't feel up to it."

"No, that's okay," said Jerry. "I'm not even swimming in a race. But maybe next time."

He unbuckled his seat belt and dashed out of the car the minute it stopped outside the school.

"I'll get a ride home with Tanya's folks," he called over his shoulder. His mother knew that Mr. and Mrs. Holman wouldn't mind dropping him off.

In the locker room, there was a lot of joking among the twenty-three boys who would be swimming that day. But there was a silent air of competitiveness just the same. Lars and Wayne kept pretty much to themselves, but Tony came over to say hello.

"Geez, I'm nervous and I'm not even racing," said Jerry.

Tony stared at him. "Hasn't Coach talked to you yet? Kevin Kincaid has the measles and can't swim the hundred-yard freestyle. I overheard the coach say he was thinking of putting you in to fill the lanes for the team!"

Jerry's heart almost stopped. "What?" he squeaked. Just then he saw Coach Fulton walking toward him.

"Jerry, I can see by your face that Kendrix here has spilled the beans. Now you've got three options. I want you to think about them carefully. One, you can refuse to swim. Two, you can swim but choose not to be officially entered in the race. Or, three, you can race officially. It's up to you."

Jerry considered what the coach had said. Not race when he had the chance? No way! But what about competing but not being counted? It was hardly worth even racing then, Jerry figured. That would be like hitting a home run but not having it show up on the scoreboard! Still . . . he'd never been in a race before. What if he made a fool of himself? Or worse, what if he came in last?

Jerry shook his head. It was a chance he'd have to take. "Count me in — all the way, Coach!" he said.

Coach Fulton looked at him thoughtfully, then nodded. "The hundred-yard freestyle is raced about halfway through the meet. Don't forget to check in. And listen carefully for your lane number when the announcer calls the race. Just swim the way you always do, Jerry, and you'll do fine." With that, he turned and left.

Sure, that's all there is to it, thought Jerry. Just a few minutes in the pool and it's all over. Tony will probably win, but I just want to place. I don't want to —

He couldn't even think of the word *lose*. Tony slapped him on the back encouragingly, but the butterflies that danced around in Jerry's stomach wouldn't calm down. He drew a deep breath and went out to the pool.

"Good afternoon, ladies and gentlemen, and welcome to the Bolton Middle School swimming pool. Today's competition features the mighty Bolton Blues in the — you guessed it — blue-on-blue swimsuits who are pitted against the red-and-gold-suited Hall Junior High Cougars."

Jerry looked down at his Bolton Blues team suit. This is it, he thought. I'm really swimming for the team.

Since his race wasn't scheduled until midway through the program, he had plenty of time to watch how the rest of the team acted. When it came time for his turn, he didn't want to make a fool of himself.

"*Our next event will be the one-hundred-yard freestyle —*"

What? Already? No, it must be a mistake. He could hardly believe that the time had come.

"*Swimming for the Blues in lane one will be Tony Kendrix, in lane three will be Randy Epstein, and in lane five, Jerry Grayson. Swimming in lane two for the Cougars will be —*"

Jerry took his position on the number 5 block. He was numb. He couldn't tell whether it was a hundred degrees or ten below zero. There was no feeling in his body whatsoever. His heart was pounding so loudly, he didn't think he'd be able to hear the starting signal.

"*On your mark!*"

There was a pause while the judges made sure everyone was in a legal position.

"*Get set!*"

Jerry thought the next pause would never end, that he would fall over in a dead faint before the gun went off.

BANG!

He unflexed his legs and dove into the pool.

When he emerged, he could hear the steady

splash of water and excited cheers of the crowd. To his horror, he realized that the other swimmers were already making their way down the lanes — and he hadn't even started swimming!

Panic-stricken, Jerry struck out wildly, slashing through the water with a choppy, uneven stroke. The race would be only four laps, and then it would be over. He had to catch up with the other competitors!

Jerry's breath came in ragged gasps as he tried to swim as fast as he could. He touched the wall at the end of the first lap and lunged around through the waves to begin the second. Suddenly, he saw something that turned his heart cold — two of the other swimmers were coming back toward him. They had already begun their third lap.

He started slicing away at the water, flipping his head each time it came out of the water, and kicking wildly behind him. After the third turn, he just wanted to finish the race. His arms felt like limp spaghetti, his legs seemed to have lead weights attached to them, and his lungs hurt so much, he thought they were going to burst open. He just managed to reach the edge of the pool where the race had started before he collapsed in the water.

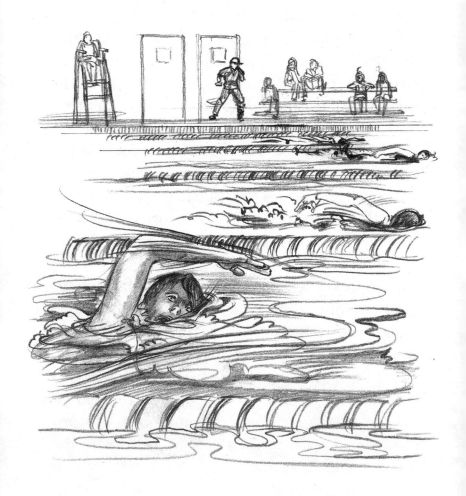

He didn't need to look up or listen to the announcer. He could tell that all the others had finished ahead of him. He was dead last. And, for one second, he almost wished that he were dead.

"The next event will be the one-hundred-yard backstroke —"

Trying not to look anyone in the eye, Jerry dragged himself out of the pool and over to the team bench. Coach Fulton was waiting for him with a towel.

"Nice work, Jerry," said the coach.

Nice work! Hah! Who was he kidding! Jerry wanted to crawl under the bench or slide down the drain in the center of the pool.

The coach went on, "I probably shouldn't have put you in without more instruction, but I thought that you'd benefit from being in a real race. It looks all too easy when you're just doing laps or watching a practice. There's a lot more to racing than a good stroke and muscle power."

"I . . . guess you're right, Coach," said Jerry. "But, you see, I think my leg is still a little weak, too. I don't think it was really up to the pressure, yet."

Jerry could tell from the look on his face that the coach didn't buy that excuse.

"Let's just say there's more work to do," Coach Fulton said. "I'll catch up with you next practice. Meanwhile, let's see what's going on in the pool. I think Tanya is about ready to compete in the hundred-yard backstroke."

They turned to the pool, where Tanya was indeed lined up for the backstroke event. She stood in the shallow water at the edge of the pool in lane three, waiting for the sounding gun.

BANG!

And off the six girls went.

The race was really close. During the third lap, it was almost impossible to see who was ahead. But during the fourth lap, the girl in lane two started to break away. Tanya kept up with her about halfway down the pool — and then lagged behind. Still, she finished strongly enough to take second place.

As disappointed as he was with his own performance, Jerry was happy for her. When she made her way over to the Blues' bench, he flipped his towel at her and called out, "Way to go!"

Tanya was so happy, her excitement seemed to spread throughout the team. Maybe that was the extra push they needed. They ended up winning the meet by a good forty points. It was their best showing that season.

But even so, Jerry didn't feel like a victor. He hadn't contributed anything to the score.

After the meet, Tanya's parents were waiting outside to drive her and Jerry home.

"How did it go?" Mrs. Holman asked.

"Pretty good," said Tanya. "I came in second in the one-hundred-yard backstroke."

"And you, Jerry," asked Mr. Holman. "Did you get a chance to swim your first race today?"

"Yeah," said Jerry, glumly. "I came in last."

"So what!" Tanya protested. "It was your first race, after all. All the other kids in that event had raced before. At least you went the distance. I've seen kids give up halfway and just leave the pool."

"Oh, sure, real losers," said Jerry.

"Sounds to me like we have a case of first-time blues," said Mr. Holman. "You'll get over it. You're a natural athlete. Well, here we are at your house, Jerry. See you at the next meet."

"I'll see you before then," said Tanya. "Like Monday at practice, okay?"

"Maybe," said Jerry. He unbuckled his seat belt and got out of the car. "Thanks for the ride."

During the rest of the weekend, Jerry avoided discussion of swimming or baseball or sports of any kind. Since it seemed to be drizzling or raining all weekend, he spent most of his time down in the cellar working on a model airplane kit. He'd started it about two years ago and hadn't touched it since.

Whenever Mr. or Mrs. Grayson tried to talk with him about the meet or anything else on his mind, he put them off.

"Telephone for you, Jerry," Mrs. Grayson called down the cellar stairs. "It's Tony Kendrix."

"I'll call him back," Jerry shouted up to her.

But he never did.

By his bedtime Sunday night, he had decided he was through with swimming. How could he have really expected to get anywhere against kids who had been working at it for so much longer? Who was he trying to fool? So what if he had a natural stroke? The coach said that wasn't enough.

But as he lay on his pillow staring up at the ceiling, he could feel the rush that had spread throughout his body when he heard the announcer.

"On your mark!"

Amazing! It felt so much like the rush he got when he stared down the line at the pitcher when he was at bat.

Maybe there was something . . . maybe swimming . . . practice . . . *get set* . . . "kick those feet!" . . .

He fell asleep dreaming of cool water swirling around his head.

The rain had stopped and a heavy mist was rising from the ground when Jerry awoke the next morning. It was hard to tell what time it was.

Six-fifteen! Of course, the house was still silent. His folks didn't get the other kids up for another half hour. Over on her dog bed across the room, Yogi stretched, yawned, and wagged her stubby tail.

"Okay, champ, we'll go for a walk. Give me a few secs," Jerry whispered.

He got dressed and slipped out the kitchen door, followed by the frisky Yogi. As he strolled down the driveway to the street, he started thinking about swimming — and baseball — one more time.

This is it, he decided. Either I really go for it and put in the effort or I quit swimming altogether. I'll just do my exercises, swim a few laps, and leave. None of this pacing or practicing or anything else.

And then, as soon as Doc says it's okay, I'll start taking batting practice. I know I'm good enough to get a shot as a replacement on the baseball team.

I know I can hit. I know I'm darn good at fielding.

Maybe that's the problem. I don't know if I can be a good swimmer. I don't know if I can win races.

He remembered something his dad had said to him a long time ago: "You'll never know until you really, really try."

8 〜〜〜〜

That afternoon, Jerry faced the pool with a new sense of determination. By the time the first person showed up, he was finished with his exercises and had started his land drill for the backstroke.

When Tanya came in and saw him at work, a big smile crossed her face.

"All right!" said Tanya, giving him the V sign.

Jerry nodded in her direction but kept on working. He was still at it when Coach Fulton stopped by.

"Stick around for a few minutes after practice today, Jerry," said the coach. "We can work on turns. And later this week, we'll improve your dive. Those are two of the areas where most beginners lose time and points."

"I'll be there," said Jerry.

And he was. When the coach signaled that official

practice was over for the day, he called out to Lars Morrison.

"Lars, come on over here," he said. "I want you to help demonstrate a flip turn for Jerry."

Lars nodded and got into the shallow end of the pool several feet in front of Jerry and the coach. At the coach's signal, Lars swam toward them. Then, just as his hand touched the wall, he somersaulted and was swimming in the opposite direction. Jerry remembered the first time he'd seen that move — and he was just as confused now as he'd been then.

For the next half hour, under the coach's guidance and Lars's example, Jerry learned how to do a complete flip turn from the crawl.

"You see, you're really doing a straight, forward somersault over onto your back, and then you twist," said the coach. "As your fingers brush the wall — which they must do, or you'll be disqualified — you begin to roll forward. And then, it's a ninety-degree twist that puts you on your side just as your feet touch the wall."

"And the minute my feet touch the wall," added Lars, "I twist the rest of the way so I'm up on the surface and already starting my stroke in the other direction."

"Wow! That's pretty complicated," said Jerry.

"Trial and error," said the coach. "Lars, you go ahead and do it first."

Lars swam out a few yards and then approached the edge of the pool doing a crawl.

Jerry watched him intently. He tried to put together in his mind what the coach had said and what Lars was doing.

Then it was his turn.

It seemed to him that he did just what he was told, but he ended up upside down, with a nose full of water. He gasped, snorted, and floundered as he regained his balance.

Lars smiled, but he wasn't mean. In fact, he said, "You almost got it. You just forgot the second twist."

When he recovered his breath, Coach Fulton gave him a minute to calm down. Then he asked him to try it again.

This time, even though it took a while and felt awkward, Jerry got it right.

"There you go," said the coach. "You're on the right track. Tony!" He called over to the long-legged swimmer sitting on the far edge of the pool talking to Tanya. "Come on over here."

When Tony arrived at the shallow end, Coach Fulton described the way he wanted Jerry to practice his turns.

"You two guys start out with Jerry about ten feet away. Swim toward the edge, and then all three of you do your turns at the same time. I want you to develop a rhythm to it that's solid and dependable, Jerry. And when you have it down, you can practice on your own. Tanya, you're not doing anything right now," he called to her. "Come on over and keep an eye on their turns. I'll be back in fifteen minutes."

The next quarter hour went like a breeze. Jerry could hardly believe how natural the turn had become after he got it right. How could he even have thought of racing until he knew stuff like this?

During the next week, Jerry managed to work in some extra coaching from Mr. Fulton, Tony, or Tanya — and even from some of the other members of the team once in a while.

After he perfected his flip turn, he learned how to dive properly.

"A long, shallow dive can cut seconds from your

time," Tanya explained. "The farther out you go, the less distance you have to swim. And if you don't have to come up from below, you can start swimming sooner. The same is true for the backstroke takeoff. Push yourself as far as possible from the wall."

And with each session, he got more and more comfortable. By the end of the week, he couldn't resist showing Tanya how well he had mastered one of his big problems.

"Just watch this takeoff!" he shouted. Then he demonstrated how well he had learned to start off in a backstroke race. As he pushed off from the side of the pool, Tanya jumped in on one side and Tony, who appeared out of nowhere, jumped in on the other. The two of them started backstroking furiously next to him, churning up a tidal wave of water in their combined wake.

But Jerry wasn't ruffled. He kept his head and continued to do exactly what he had learned. When he touched the opposite edge of the pool, Wayne Cabot shouted down to the three of them.

"The winner by a good palm and a half, Jerry Grayson!"

The winner — Jerry Grayson! It sounded great.

Deep down, he knew that he would love to hear those words in a real race.

Tony had scrambled out of the pool and was stomping up and down.

"Oh, no," he cried in mock misery. "I've been beaten by that gimpy lump of quicksand Jerry Grayson!"

"Me, too," cried Tanya, in the pool. "What's left for us in this world?"

"There's nothing!" said Tony. He walked over to the diving board and strode boldly to the edge. "Good-bye cruel world!"

He pinched his nose, bounced high up, and leaped off in a cannonball.

As a huge wall of water rose and began to descend, all the others in his vicinity began splashing water in his direction and calling out, "Jerry! Jerry!"

He knew they were teasing — and he loved every minute of it.

"I don't believe it!" Mr. Grayson banged his fist down on the newspaper in front of him.

"What's the matter, dear? The stock market

crash?" asked Mrs. Grayson, seated on the other end of the couch.

"No, look at who the Yankees traded!" He pushed the sports section of the newspaper over to her.

She pored over the picture and the column that filled a quarter of a page. Then she looked up and asked, "Jerry?"

Jerry was playing tug-of-war with Yogi. The feisty schnauzer had clenched a rubber dog toy and wouldn't let go of it. Jerry dropped his end and looked up.

"What?" he replied.

"Aren't you even interested in what's going on in spring practice? Your father just mentioned the Yankees' big trade today."

"I heard about it on TV a little while ago," he said, but he made no other comment about the big news in professional baseball.

Mr. and Mrs. Grayson stared at each other. This was really unusual for Jerry. He was generally a walking encyclopedia of baseball information. News about something happening on one of the major league teams usually started him off on a long talk.

Instead, he got up and stretched. "I think I'll hit the hay a little early tonight. We've got a full practice tomorrow."

"Batting practice?" asked Mrs. Grayson.

"No, swimming," said Jerry.

He gave his parents good-night kisses and, followed by the faithful Yogi, he went up to his room.

Jerry didn't know it, but after he left, Mr. Grayson shook his head.

And Mrs. Grayson whispered across the room, "Is it my imagination, or is his hair turning a little green?"

On Wednesday morning, Mrs. Grayson reminded Jerry that he had a final doctor's appointment for his leg that afternoon. Doctor Gold and Bob Fulton had been keeping each other informed of Jerry's progress. So when classes had finished for the day, Jerry headed for the doctor's office instead of the pool.

To his delight, Doctor Gold gave him a clean bill of health. His bones had completely healed. The muscles were well on their way to full strength.

"It looks like the swimming has helped," she said. "But now that you're okay, maybe you'll go back to baseball?"

Jerry was silent for a moment. He couldn't deny

that being able to play baseball again was the first thought that had crossed his mind.

But the more he thought about it, the more he realized how committed he had become to swimming. So he turned to Doctor Gold and said, "Throw away all that practice time and hard work to sit on the bench during baseball season? No way! Besides, there's always next year for baseball."

Jerry left the doctor's office happier than he'd felt for a long time. But suddenly the whole afternoon seemed empty. He hadn't realized how much he'd begun to schedule his life around swimming practice.

He decided to head for home and tell his mother the good news about his leg. He was halfway there when he heard footsteps behind him. He turned to see who it was.

Tanya ran up next to him and stopped, breathless.

"I've been chasing you for the last four blocks," she panted. "Stop, already!"

"I don't know if you're ever going to make a long-distance sprinter," he said, joking.

"Go ahead and laugh," she said. "But I have some hot news for you. I checked the bulletin board outside Coach Fulton's office. And —" she paused dramatically.

"And — come on!" Jerry said impatiently.

"And I saw the roster for the meet against the Clapham Clippers next week. The coach has you down for two different events!"

"He does?"

"Yes!" she said, nodding. "You know what that means, don't you?"

"I . . . I think so," he replied, hesitatingly. He was almost afraid to say it out loud.

But Tanya wasn't. "It means you're a full-fledged member of the swimming team now!"

9 〜〜〜〜

Jerry was so excited that he hadn't even asked Tanya which two events the coach had him down for. But he soon found out. He was scheduled to swim the one-hundred-yard freestyle and the two-hundred-yard freestyle.

"So what's wrong with my butterfly? With my breaststroke?" he asked.

"Don't be a ninny," she said. "Those are two terrific events. You should be happy as . . . as a . . ."

"Happy as a shark at a clambake?" he suggested.

"No, more like a jellyfish at a jamboree," she said.

"A what?"

"Jelly? *Jam* — bo-ree? Get it?"

"Oh, that's awful!" he groaned. "I'd better get on my way before you come out with any more."

"Okay," she said. "See you at practice."

"Hey, Tanya," he called after her. "Thanks for the good news."

From that moment on, Jerry poured himself into his swimming practice. He was pleased his extra effort learning how to do flip turns and racing dives had paid off. Still, he knew he wouldn't be content to swim short-distance freestyle events for the rest of the season. Lars, Wayne, and Sammy Wu had the breaststroke spots filled, and he still didn't feel comfortable with the butterfly. That left the backstroke.

So, in addition to perfecting his flip turns and dives, Jerry started concentrating on his backstroke drills a little more each day. The very first thing he did when he got in the pool was swim lap after lap.

As he pushed off from the edge of the pool, he checked what he had been taught by Coach Fulton and the other coaches during previous practices.

Arm over arm. Check.

Six kicks to a two-arm cycle. Check.

Extra push when the arm was stretched full-length just past the head. Check.

Slice the water with the little finger first. Check.

Pull the arm through the water deep — and push through at the thigh. Check.

Stroke by stroke, he ploughed his way down the lane until his outstretched fingertips touched the opposite wall. And then it was time for the backstroke turn that he had learned after a lot of hard work.

As soon as his hand touched the pool wall, he snapped his head backward and downward, arched his back, and brought up his knees into a kind of underwater somersault. Tony had shown him how to give himself a little bit of a twist after that to help settle into a proper backstroke position after the turn. Then, when his feet hit the wall, he stretched his right arm back for a strong starting stroke as he pushed off with both feet.

Whew! It was hard work, but he knew it was the only way he could make any headway with the backstroke. All the practice was starting to pay off.

"Nice going."

"Looking good, there."

"Good turn. Way to go."

As he got to know them, other members of the team were generous with their praise — and their help. He didn't always have to wait for Tony or Tanya to do laps. It seemed as though someone was always there to join him when he was ready to practice his crawl.

"Your crawl isn't exactly the way the textbooks show it," said Coach Fulton. "But since it works so well for you, I think we'll leave it alone and build on strength. But, remember, like I told you before, there's a lot more than just a good stroke to winning a race."

"Gotcha," said Jerry. Coach Fulton never seemed to run out of patience — except when he felt someone wasn't doing his or her best — or, worse, didn't play by the rules.

"Just like every sport," he'd explain to newcomers like Jerry, "swimming has its rules. The sooner you learn them and the better you learn them, the more you'll get out of swimming."

So Jerry toed the mark. He played by the rules at practice and kept them in mind when he was working out on his own.

And he did get better and better and stronger and stronger. By the end of the week, he felt ready for the meet.

✿   ✿   ✿

When he got out of bed on the morning of the meet, Jerry automatically checked the weather. It was cloudy and looked like it might rain later.

Then it dawned on him that the weather didn't matter. It wasn't like baseball. He was going to be swimming at an indoor pool.

Still, he felt the same rush of excitement that always struck him on the day of a big baseball game. There was something at stake today, too. The swimming meet was another form of competition — and he was going to be an official part of it.

The meet was scheduled to take place at the school pool. When he got there, he could see the visiting team's bus parked outside. On the outside there was a big black-and-gold banner that said "Ridgeway Rams." He remembered playing against the Little League team from Ridgeway a few years ago. The Bolton Little Leaguers had won that game.

And we're going to win this one, too, he said to himself.

The first person Jerry saw in the locker room was Tony.

"How're you doing, slugger?" asked Tony. Somehow or other, Jerry's fondness for baseball had become known. A lot of the guys on the team had started using that nickname. It always made Jerry smile.

"I'm okay," Jerry answered.

"Oh, yeah?" said Tony. "So how come you've spun the dial on your combination lock about fifty times? And I still don't see you opening it."

Jerry grinned at him sheepishly. "I guess I am just a little nervous," he admitted.

"Good," said Tony. "Shows you're human."

"Yeah, some of the guys were beginning to wonder," said Lars, who had been sitting nearby. "As a matter of fact —"

"Don't start in on him," said Tony. "It's Jerry's first official meet, so we have to go easy. We'll take care of the slugger here after we win the meet."

"Let's go, Blues!"

The cheers rang out as the team left the locker room and entered the pool area.

Coach Fulton was talking to some of the other guys on the team. Then he came over to Jerry.

"Are you all set?" he asked.

"I think so," Jerry replied.

"Okay, just relax then until your event is announced," said the coach. "Then get out there and do the best you can. That's all I ask."

But that's not all I want to do, Jerry said to himself. I want to do well enough to score some points for the team. I want to show everyone that I have learned a thing or two.

He stepped into the water and splashed around for a few seconds. Then he did some exercises to loosen up a little.

"Testing — one — two — three."

The sound coming over the loudspeakers quieted everyone down.

Jerry climbed out of the pool and went over to the Blues bench. He toweled off as the announcer greeted everyone and introduced the officials who would be judging the events at the meet. Then, along with everyone else, Jerry stood and sang the "Star Spangled Banner." Deep in the back of his mind, he could almost hear an umpire shout, "Play ball!"

Okay, he thought, he would play ball — but in the cool, green water of a swimming pool.

It didn't take long for the first few events to be run. The Bolton team held its own, and the score-board showed only a slight lead for the Rams.

And then it was time for the boys hundred-yard freestyle.

"Swimmers, please take your places," said the announcer.

Jerry was swimming in lane three, smack in the middle of the pool.

Maybe I'll get lost in all the splashing on either side, he thought for a second. Then, he caught himself. What kind of an attitude is that? I'm going to be right in the thick of it and I'm going to give it all I can — for the team!

He climbed up on the starting block and shook loose some of the tension. Then he positioned himself for the dive.

Just four laps, he said to himself. Just four — but I have to pace them. And I have to remember everything I've learned.

"On your mark . . . get set . . . BANG!

At the sound of the gun, he sprang forth and dove into the water. He remembered to keep it shallow for a quick return to the surface — and then to start his crawl immediately.

The lesson was well learned. Jerry could tell that he was right up there with the swimmers on either side by the time he was midway down the pool for the first lap.

And then he reached the end of the pool and went into his turn. It was swift and smooth — and quickly put him back on track for the next lap.

In the distance, he could hear the noise of the crowd and the sound of the loudspeaker, but he paid no attention to it. Just do everything you've learned, he kept saying to himself over and over.

He tried to ignore the Rams swimmers on either side. Still, he could tell that he had gotten a little bit ahead of both of them.

For one second, it flashed through his mind that he might be the leader, that he might just win the event. But he quickly slammed the door shut on that thought and kept up his stroke, nice and steady.

Going into the last lap, he was clearly ahead of the Ram swimmer in lane two by several lengths, and a little bit ahead of the competing Ram in lane four. It was time to put on the steam.

Jerry took deep, measured breaths as he extended his arms in front of him, powerfully slicing his way through the water. In careful, timed sequence, he kicked his legs, churning up a wake that helped to propel him forward faster and faster. With each stroke, he tried a little harder to go a little faster as the pressure within his body expanded.

And then he felt the tips of the fingers on his right hand touch the tile at the end of the pool. The race was over.

For a second, Jerry expected to see the water filled with steam all around him. He gasped as he caught his breath, holding on to the side of the pool. In the distance, he could just hear the announcer's voice.

"The winner of the one-hundred-yard freestyle in lane five for the Bolton Blues was Ace Willoughby —"

Ace! Good for him, thought Jerry, splashing some water on his face to cool off. That's one for the good guys!

"In second place, also for the Blues, in lane three, was Jerry Grayson."

Another one for the Blues, hey, that's great, thought Jerry. Hey! Wait a minute! That's me! I came in second!

He leaped out of the pool and dashed over to the Blues bench. Ace was the first one to slap a high five on him.

"Nice going, slugger," he said.

"Nice going, yourself," said Jerry. He was almost as happy for Ace as he was for himself.

"Settle down, you two," said the coach after he had congratulated all the guys who had just finished the hundred. "Rest up, there isn't that much time until the two hundred."

Jerry was really revved up now. For the first time, he felt the taste of success as a swimmer. Sure it was only a short race. Sure it was his best stroke. But he still had placed in the top three — in the top two, for that matter. He knew he was headed in the right direction.

But he settled himself down and tried to concentrate on the next event he'd be swimming. The two-hundred-yard freestyle wasn't just double the distance; it called for a lot more discipline. The increases in his output had to be more gradual, but more powerful if he were to make any headway. He knew that the coaches often saved their best swimmers for just one or two big races like the two hundred.

Paul Prescott and Kevin Kincaid, who had gotten over the measles, would be swimming in the two hundred for the Bolton team along with him. When the event was announced, they clapped their arms around him as they left the bench.

This time Jerry discovered that he was swimming in lane six. He'd have just one competitor on one side. The tiled wall of the pool and the fans above would be on his other side.

Hope it doesn't make me lopsided, he thought to himself, grinning.

As he stepped up on the diving stand at lane six, he felt really comfortable. After all, he'd been in a race just a few minutes ago. There was nothing to it. All he had to do was swim eight laps. Eight! That was twice as many as he had just finished swimming.

Suddenly, all the fears buried deep down in the pit of his stomach rose up. Would he measure up? Was the hundred just a fluke? Or would he be able to swim well enough to help out the team?

Jerry knew what he had to do. He had to swim the race exactly the way the coach had taught him. There was no room for any mistakes.

BANG!

Jerry unflexed his knees and dove into the water

straight ahead. He cut through its surface like a sleek surfboard and started to swim.

One strong arm forged its way through the cold green water as the other forced the backwater away like a powerful paddle wheel.

He kept his breathing steady as his head emerged from the water with each stroke. There were no extra flips, no unnecessary motions. He cut his way through the water like a well-oiled machine.

Alongside, the swimmer in lane five had stayed with him lap after lap until midway through the race. As he headed into his fifth lap, Jerry could see the distance opening up between the two of them as he took the lead.

But what was happening in the other lanes? There was no way to tell.

Jerry remembered what the coach had told him way back: never mind the announcer or anything else. Swim your own race.

That was exactly what he did. Lap by lap he stretched himself further and further. Stroke after stroke, his powerful arms never let up. Both legs kept up a steady kick, helping to propel him faster and faster through the water. His whole body responded in perfect sequence at the turns, and his lungs seemed to expand more and more to contain the deeper and deeper breaths he had to take on the way to the finish.

And then it was over. He could hear the shouts from the stands as the Ridgeway and Bolton fans broke out into loud cheers.

Before the public address system could make the announcement, Jerry knew that something special had happened. Paul and Kevin had come rushing over to him while he was still in the water, and Coach Fulton was approaching with a smile that went from ear to ear. The whole Bolton team was jumping up and down at the bench.

Finally, the sound of the announcer's voice broke through the rest of the noise, and he could hear:

"The winner of the boys two-hundred-yard freestyle is Jerry Grayson —"

He had won! He had come in first!

Jerry managed to work his way over to the Bolton bench, where everyone couldn't wait to lay high fives or tens on him, hug him, or just shout congratulations in his ear.

But the meet wasn't over. As Jerry sat down to watch the rest of the events, he glowed with an inner pride. He had proved that he could compete in this new, exciting sport — and that he had what it took to win.

Still, he knew that he hadn't completely conquered swimming.

There was another thought hidden way, way in the back of his mind. It was definitely something he didn't want to discuss with Tony or Tanya or anyone else on the team. And not even Coach Fulton, yet.

Secretly, he wanted to compete in the five-hundred-yard freestyle. The way Jerry looked at it, that was the big test. It was the longest distance, and it took the strongest swimmers to even enter the event.

Sure, Coach Fulton had said he had a good crawl — but it probably wasn't ready for the big time yet. He would simply have to keep at it.

"How many laps is that?" Tanya asked one morning as she stepped into the pool. He had just finished his longest distance so far — fifteen laps back and forth. That was the same as 375 yards.

"Oh, who knows?" he replied. "I don't bother counting sometimes." It was just a little fib, he thought. No real harm done.

"You should get into the habit," she said. Without another word, she plunged forward and began to do the butterfly down the lane at the opposite side of the pool.

By the end of the week, he was able to go the full distance for the five hundred. And a few sessions later, he started feeling pretty good about it. Still, with so little experience, he could hardly broach the subject to Coach Fulton.

"Are you practicing your backstroke on your own?" asked the coach one day.

"Every day I do at least a few laps," answered Jerry.

"Good," said Coach Fulton. "What about the others? Breaststroke? Butterfly?"

"I, uh, I do them in regular team practice," said Jerry.

"All right," said the coach, nodding. "Just want to make sure you're getting an all-around education here."

"What about my crawl, you know, for the freestyle?" asked Jerry. "Aren't you going to ask me about that?"

"Don't worry," said the coach. "I've been keeping my eye on your crawl. I can tell that you're getting enough practice there."

"I . . . I, uh, I had a question," said Jerry. "I was wondering if, maybe, I could try out for the five hundred."

"The five hundred?" asked the coach. "That's a big step. I don't know if you're ready for that yet, Jerry."

"I've been practicing on my own, Coach," Jerry said. "I really think I can help out the team in that event."

"Let me think about it," said the coach. "And I'll put you into a practice race, just to see how you do. We'll take it from there."

"Uh, Mom," said Jerry, tying up the stack of newspapers in front of him, "would you mind if I was a little late for dinner tonight? I want to put in some extra time at the Y this afternoon, and the only time the pool's available is just before dinner."

"Jerry, I'm starting to look for fins," said Mrs.

Grayson. "You spend so much time in the water, you're beginning to turn into a fish, I think!"

"Is that a yes?" Jerry asked.

"Well, it isn't exactly a no," she said. "But one half hour — and not a minute more."

"By the way, what are we having for dinner?" he asked.

"Fishcakes," she said, with a smile.

"Okay, have the following six boys line up for the five hundred freestyle," said Coach Fulton one afternoon. He called out the names, one by one, until he came to the final spot.

"Jerry Grayson."

Several heads turned in his direction. Tanya glanced over at Tony as if to ask, "Did you know Jerry was up for the five hundred?"

Tony just shook his head.

Just as the six swimmers got into position for the start of the race, a loud wailing siren was heard over the speaker system.

"Oh, no," groaned Tanya. "A fire drill!"

"What if it's a real fire?" asked a girl sitting next to her.

"We could all jump into the pool!" suggested another girl.

Coach Fulton blew his whistle and shouted, "Let's all leave the way we've practiced!"

They filed out in an orderly way through the locker room, grabbing their gym bags on the way. As soon as they got outside the building, they threw on shoes, jackets, pants, or whatever minimum clothing they needed.

The drill took about twenty minutes — long enough to put an end to swimming practice for that day.

"There's no time to post the final roster," Coach Fulton said. "So I'll just announce any changes to the usual lineup on Saturday. See you then."

With the next meet scheduled for the day after tomorrow, Jerry was left hanging.

Will I get another shot at the five hundred? he wondered. Or was that my only chance?

10 ≋≋≋

"You won't forget," said Jerry. He swallowed the last mouthful of the milk in his glass. "You're all coming to the meet. I'll see you afterward?"

"We won't," said his father. "Don't worry, we'll all be there. Right, kids?"

"Right," said David.

"Yup," said Lucie.

"And you, too, Mom, right?"

"Of course," said Mrs. Grayson. She handed him his gym bag. "Now just try to relax. This isn't your first race, you know."

He nodded. But inside his stomach, there were flip-flops all over the place. It wasn't his first race, but it was the first one his whole family would attend.

Gulp! What if he made a fool of himself?

On the other hand, he thought, it wasn't as if he hadn't ever been under pressure before. What about the Little League playoffs, when he made the final out by leaping half a mile into the air for that incredible catch? That was pressure.

Face it, he said to himself, I'm an athlete. Athletes live with pressure. So what's another couple of races?

And then he thought about the five hundred. Would Coach Fulton put him in instead of one of his regulars?

The flip-flops started all over.

On the bus to the meet, the coach called for quiet.

"Let's hold it down," he said. "I have a few announcements."

He ran through the listing of all the swimmers in the various events. Jerry had been pulled from the one-hundred-yard freestyle and the two-hundred-yard freestyle.

Did this mean he wasn't going to swim at all? Wasn't he a member of the team?

The coach continued to go over the rest of the events until he came to the five-hundred-yard boys freestyle.

Again, the sixth name on the list was Jerry's!

That was it — all or nothing. The coach was letting him swim the one big race that he had asked for.

Okay, thought Jerry. I'll show him. I'll show everyone I have what it takes.

Then he remembered that his whole family would be sitting in the stands. What would they think? Would they understand why he wasn't in the other events? Would they realize that he was being saved for the one big race?

Yeah, that's it — he was the coach's secret weapon. Coach Fulton was counting on him. He wouldn't let him down.

But as the whole team stood for the playing of the "Star Spangled Banner," Jerry felt those flip-flops return to his stomach.

Tony must have noticed that he was ghost white. The curly-haired swimmer moved over next to him on the bench and said, "Deep breaths, real slow."

"What?" asked Jerry.

"Lower your head a little, and take just a few deep breaths," said Tony. "It helps me when I do that. You know, get rid of that funny feeling in my stomach."

Jerry didn't say a word. He just dropped his head and started breathing deeply.

"Our next event will be the boys one-hundred-yard freestyle," said the announcer over the loud-speaker.

That's the one I could have been in, thought Jerry. But Tony's in it. I'll root for him.

"Come on, Tony!" he shouted during the final lap when the top two swimmers were coming down to the finish. It was so close, he couldn't tell from where he sat. But the judges soon made the announcement. The winner was Tony Kendrix!

Jerry was really glad for him. At the same time, his competitive juices were stirred. He hoped he would do as well in the big five-oh-oh.

Tanya was entered in the girls one-hundred-yard butterfly. She'd been working very hard on this stroke for the last few weeks and it had paid off in a big way. There was no wait for a call from the judges. Everyone could tell she had won. A loud cheer rose from the stands as she raised her fist in the victory sign.

There was only one more event before the five

hundred. This was the two-hundred-yard boys backstroke. Both Lars and Wayne would swim for the Blues in this one. They were both such favorites, it might as well be a two-man race.

BANG!

They were off!

During the first two laps, they were just about even, stroke for stroke, with only one swimmer from the other team giving them any competition. Swimming in lane three, right between Lars in lane two and Wayne in lane four, was Paddy O'Malley.

Paddy kept up a close second place all the way, even though he probably knew that he'd end up in third. Still, he never quit trying.

As they came down to the wire in the eighth and final lap, it was still a duel between Lars and Wayne for first.

And then, Wayne seemed to stop cold in the middle of the pool. His body twisted and he splashed around, treading water as all the others passed him by. Then he made his way to the edge of the pool, where Coach Fulton and a few of the guys helped him crawl out.

"Cramp," explained Tony. "Poor guy."

"Is that what happened?" asked Jerry.

"Yeah, some guys get 'em all the time," said Tony. "Some only once in a while. Some never. I've been lucky." He made it clear he didn't want to discuss it any more by turning away and staring at the scoreboard.

Lars had won easily, and Paddy O'Malley was the proud possessor of second place.

A flash of concern for Wayne ran through Jerry's mind until he saw him walking about normally. Wayne would be in a lot more races and take a few first places from Lars, Jerry expected.

"The next event will be the boys five-hundred-yard freestyle," said the announcer. *"Swimming in lane one for the Clapham Clippers will be Fred 'Flash' Gordon; in lane three, Danny Chang; and in lane five, Silvio Reppuci. For the Blues, in lane two, Albie 'Ace' Willoughby; in lane four, Paul Prescott; and in lane six, Jerry Grayson. Swimmers, please take your places."*

Jerry felt as if he had lead weights attached to the bottom of his feet as he walked over to the starting block for lane six. He hardly noticed that it was right next to the stands where his family had found seats.

But as he put his first foot onto the block, he heard his little sister, Lucie, shout out, "Come on, Jerry! Let's see you win!"

The little pipsqueak of a voice cutting through all the noise of the crowd must have tickled a few ribs. A whole section of the crowd started laughing.

I hope they're not laughing at me, thought Jerry. He patted his stomach to settle those flip-flops that had started up again. I *really* hope they won't be laughing at me after the race!

He knew that Paul Prescott was the big favorite. He'd been swimming the five hundred all year. But Ace Willoughby had only started swimming the five hundred after winning the last three of his two hundreds. This was his third five hundred.

Jerry hadn't been swimming long enough to be able to size up the competition on the other side. The Clapham Clippers were a bunch of unknowns to him.

What difference did it make? he asked himself as he stood there waiting for the starting signal. Do your best, that's the most important thing. By this time, practice should have been enough to make that second nature. All he had to do was hit that water clean and start swimming his natural crawl as soon as possible. That's what had gotten him here in the first place, after all.

"All right, swimmers, on your mark!"

Jerry's toes clenched over the edge of the block. He stood there with his feet a few inches apart, his legs bent slightly at the knees. His arms were extended backward, with the palms turned upward.

"Get set!"

He leaned forward, ready to make his plunge.

BANG!

Jerry pushed off and forward at the same time. His arms swung in front of him as he entered the water a few inches below the surface.

The minute he felt the sensation of cold liquid on his fingertips, he put all his training into effect and began the six-beat crawl at a steady pace.

Then a loud whistle shrieked, and he knew right away that something was wrong. Someone had false-started.

The whistle kept blowing. The six swimmers stopped and returned to the starting position.

He glanced over at his folks in the stand. Someone seated next to them was explaining what had happened.

I guess they didn't expect a false start, thought Jerry. Neither did I. At least no one is pointing the finger at me.

But it took a little of the wind out of his sails. The next time the starting gun was fired, there was just a little less spring in his dive. Still, he hit the water cleanly and began to work his way down his lane for the first of the twenty laps it would take to complete the five hundred.

Arm over arm, stroke after stroke, he reached forward and sliced his way through the water. He tried to keep his breathing as regular as his strokes, turning his head under the water to exhale through his nose with each lap.

Nice and steady, he said to himself during the first five laps. Keep your mind on what you're doing. Reach ahead toward the end of the lane. Never mind what's going on at either side.

Still, there was no way he could miss the stroke-for-stroke splashes that accompanied him back and forth. It seemed as though the swimmer in the lane next to him was gaining a little after the third lap.

As Jerry made his fifth turn to start the sixth lap, he knew that the race was one-fourth over. It was time for him to increase his effort a little bit to make sure he wasn't falling behind. So, keeping the same rhythm between his arm strokes and his kicking, he speeded up both ever so slightly.

The swimmer on his side was just about a stroke ahead of him. Still, Jerry knew that he had to keep swimming exactly as he was, to conserve some energy for the last big push.

"As we approach the halfway mark, with ten laps to go, the leader is Silvio Repucci in lane five by just half a stroke —"

Hey, I must be right behind the leader, thought Jerry. I'm in second place and the race isn't half over yet.

"Coming on strong in lane two, however, is Ace Willoughby in second place —"

Not quite second, I guess, Jerry realized. The disappointment caused him to break his stride for a second, but he quickly recovered.

"And making a big push for third place, it looks like a tie so far between Paul Prescott and Jerry Grayson."

All right, it wasn't over yet.

Just before he reached the edge of the pool for his

tenth turn, he saw Tony crouched down holding a cardboard sign marked with a big "10" under the water for him to see. Without wasting time staring, Jerry could tell that Tony was right there cheering him on.

Second half, time to put on some more pressure. Jerry felt like he had a gearshift inside him, just like the one his dad had in his car. He'd been in first and second gear, and it was time to move into third.

Now, at each turn, at the opposite end of the pool from where the race had started, there were lap signs waiting for him. He noticed that Wayne held the fourteenth lap sign and Lars the fifteenth. Coach Fulton wanted his swimmers to know the whole team was with them.

Only five laps to go, thought Jerry. Here's where I really have to make the final push. Okay, fourth gear, here we come. He pushed off extra hard, pleased to see that both legs were still holding up fine. There was no sign that his right leg was any the worse for the pressure of the long-distance race.

"With just three laps to go, only seventy-five yards left in this race, it looks like Ace Willoughby in lane two by four strokes; making a strong push, however,

is Danny Chang in lane three; Silvio Reppuci, the early leader, has dropped down to third place; and trailing him by a — well, about a nose — is new-comer Jerry Grayson."

Fourth! He wasn't going to settle for that. He'd show them. He'd pour it on and take — well, he certainly wanted to end up in one of the top three spots. He knew he could do it.

Tony was back holding up the sign that told him it was the eighteenth lap. Jerry saw him, then rushed into his turn. He barely finished his somersault before he started to twist back into crawl position. His push-off from the wall was awkward, and he knew that he'd lost a few seconds and distance behind the leaders.

The only way to make up for it was to swim full out for both of the last laps, instead of sprinting in just the twentieth.

Jerry went for it.

11 〜〜〜〜

The flip-flops in Jerry's stomach had long since disappeared. They were now replaced with a burning sensation down in his chest. He tried to draw the air in rapidly and let it out at the exact time his head went below the water's surface. But as he stretched his arms overhead to make his way swiftly through the water, his breathing became more and more of a challenge.

The water, too, seemed to have changed. When the race began, the light, clear fluid had offered little resistance. Now it seemed to be more like thick, tough, gray motor oil that dragged down his arms as he made his way down the final two laps.

At this point, the announcer's voice was drowned out by the shouting from the stands. He heard his name and all the others amid the whistles, cheers, and general noise that floated above his head.

Every muscle in his body strained to propel him forward — and every one of those muscles cried out in pain as they were stretched to their utmost limit.

And then it was over.

The fingers of his outstretched right hand touched the edge of the pool, just below the watchful eyes of a judge with a clipboard.

Jerry couldn't tell whether he had come in first, second, or third — but he knew he wasn't last. As he lifted his body up from the water, he could tell that the swimmer in lane one, Flash Gordon, had trailed him by at least half a lap and was just now finishing.

Well, at least I wasn't a complete bust, Jerry thought, as he stood there with his chest pounding, trying to cool off.

There was still so much noise and cheering, no one seemed to know how the race had turned out. Jerry made his way out of the pool and over to the Blues bench, where his teammates had gathered around its three contenders.

"There's some sort of a problem, I think," said

Tony, wrapping a towel around Jerry. "But you did great. You should be real pleased."

"*Attention, please,*" came the announcer's voice. "*We have a disqualification in the five hundred boys freestyle. For failure to make contact properly at the end of a lap, the swimmer in lane five has been disqualified. The winner of the five-hundred-yard freestyle was Paul Prescott of the Bolton Blues!*"

The Bolton bench and fans exploded into loud cheering.

"*In second place, was Danny Chang in lane three.*"

This time, the Clapham bench led the cheering.

"*And in third place, was lane two, Ace Willoughby, followed by lane six, Jerry Grayson, and lane one, Flash Gordon.*"

Everyone now applauded briefly as the meet continued.

Jerry stood there numb with disappointment.

Fourth! And it could have been worse. Silvio was ahead of me most of the race. If he hadn't been disqualified, I might have come in fifth! Maybe that Gordon kid had a cramp, or I wouldn't have even beaten him. Who am I kidding? I shouldn't have been in this race, he thought.

Coach Fulton had congratulated Paul and Ace. He made his way over to Jerry, who had clutched the towel around him and was trying to bury his face in its folds.

The coach reached forward, found his hand, and forced a handshake out of the reluctant swimmer.

"Jerry, you should be pleased with yourself. I had my doubts about putting you in, but I'm not in the least sorry that I did," he said.

"You're not?" Jerry asked. "Even though I didn't do that well, I mean, fourth."

"I have my own standards, Jerry," said the coach. "At this point, standings shouldn't matter to you so much. You have to learn to evaluate your own performance against how well you know you can do. That's what counts."

"I guess you're right, Coach," Jerry said.

"So you made a few mistakes," said the coach. "You can learn to correct them and do better next time."

Next time. Those two words lifted Jerry's spirits a little. But mistakes? What had he done wrong?

It looked as though the coach had read his mind. "Don't worry," he said. "We'll go over everything in practice. Let's just watch the rest of the meet."

But Jerry itched to know where he had messed up. He squeezed in next to Tony on the bench and said, "Hey, Tony, I was wondering —"

But Tony held him off. "Look, Jerry, I'm swimming the backstroke in the one-hundred-yard medley relay. I have to concentrate."

Jerry could tell that he'd get nowhere asking anyone else while the meet was still taking place. He decided to hold off.

When it was over, the Blues had won another competition by a wide margin. The whole team was in great spirits as they left the locker room. Jerry tried to act cheerful, but he wasn't looking forward to seeing his family outside. He slung his gym bag over his shoulder and trailed the others into the fresh air.

"Way to go!" said Mr. Grayson, hugging him around the shoulder right away.

"You were terrific," agreed Mrs. Grayson, kissing him on the cheek.

Even Lucie seemed proud of him. She hugged his

leg and said, "I saw you swimming back and forth for a long time. Weren't you tired?"

Jerry smiled at her and nodded. "A lot," he said.

David gave him a friendly punch on the arm and said, "I was worried when you didn't swim in the events you were supposed to. But then I figured the coach was saving you for something special. The five hundred, wow!"

The whole family was so happy for him, Jerry couldn't let them know how disappointed he was in how he had finished. Fourth place. It still stuck in his throat. But he felt he had to say something about it.

"I . . . I just wish I'd ended up better," he said softly.

"Hah! You've done a lot worse," said David right off. "Remember when you struck out three times in that Little League playoff game?"

"Or the time you threw your mitt instead of the ball in the game with the Plattstown Panthers?" said his mother, with a big smile.

His father started laughing. "I think the funniest was when you swung the bat so hard you got in a twist and ended up almost knocking yourself out."

At the memory of that particular goofy move, even

Jerry couldn't keep from laughing. The whole family was still chuckling as they made their way to the car.

"Mom, I'll have my dessert later," said Jerry. "Tony and Tanya are coming over. If there's any pie left, is it okay if I give them some?"

"Of course," she answered. "And if David doesn't make a pig of himself, there will be some left over."

"Oink," said David.

"Never mind," said Mr. Grayson. "You and Lucie put these dishes in the dishwasher. And when you're through, come on in to the living room. We'll leave the kitchen for Jerry and his friends."

Briiing!

The doorbell announced the arrival of Tanya, who had a small container of vanilla ice cream.

"I thought we could have a treat," she said. "To celebrate your first five hundred."

"Great," said Jerry. "We have some pie to go with it." Before he could tell her he didn't think his performance in the five hundred was much to rave about, Tony arrived.

"Pie à la mode," he said. "My favorite." He didn't

waste time helping himself to a large scoop of ice cream and a sizable wedge of pie.

When they had finished eating, Jerry came right to the point. "So where did I mess up?" he asked.

"Didn't the coach say he'd go over it with you?" asked Tanya.

"He did," said Jerry. "But I figured the sooner I knew the better."

"You put too much pressure on yourself," said Tony.

"During the race?" asked Jerry.

"No, now!" said Tony. "You have to learn to relax once in a while."

"Leave the swimming in the pool, Jerry," said Tanya. "Believe me, the coach will go over every detail. It's incredible how he remembers these things."

"So, you aren't going to give me any clues?" Jerry asked.

"Not a one," said Tony.

"All right, I want my pie back," said Jerry.

"What?" cried two voices at the same time.

"You heard me," said Jerry, trying to keep from smiling.

"You know what?" said Tanya. "We *ought* to give it back to him. You know how?"

Tony pointed with his finger toward his open mouth, his tongue hanging out.

She nodded.

"You're both disgusting," said Jerry. "But let's finish off the ice cream anyhow."

When Jerry finally found himself alone with Coach Fulton at the pool, he discovered that none of his mistakes were big ones.

"You were thrown by the false start," said the coach. "And your next start was a little weaker. Swimming isn't like tennis. If you make a mistake the first time, you don't have to be cautious the next time. Go for it with as much zip as if it were the very beginning — because it is."

Jerry hated to admit it, but he knew the coach was right.

"Another thing," Coach Fulton went on. "You're listening to the announcer too much — instead of swimming your own race. You know about pacing. We've talked a lot about it. But you rushed headlong into the last two laps and threw away a lot of what you had gained. You might even have won that race, even after a slightly weak start."

I might have won! Jerry thought.

"But don't beat up on yourself too much," said the coach. "You were a little rough on the turns, too. And you still need to work on your breathing. Remember that exercise I taught you? Have you been practicing it?"

Jerry had to admit he hadn't. Breathing was something you did naturally, he'd thought. Why waste time on something like that?

"Listen, I want you to go all the way back to the basics," said the coach. "Do your land drills, your kicking drills, your turns, your breathing exercises, all of it. And I don't want you to spend a lot of time practicing the crawl by doing laps. There's a lot more for you to learn."

"There is?" asked Jerry.

"You still haven't swum a backstroke race yet," said the coach. "And what about your breaststroke? And your butterfly? If you're going to become an all-around swimmer, you have get those down, too."

Jerry stared at him wide-eyed.

"And you have to be an all-around swimmer before you can even think of really making a mark in this sport. You have the potential to be a great swimmer. Don't waste it."

The coach moved on to a group of girls who were practicing their flip turns.

"That's it, push!" the coach shouted.

But all Jerry heard was *"You have the potential to be a great swimmer."*

The words were carved indelibly in his mind.

12 〰〰〰〰

The coach's words rang in Jerry's ears throughout the weekend. By Monday, he realized he had to learn to do everything — and he had to learn to do it well.

He worked out a schedule of private training in addition to team practice and showed it to the coach. It included an extra half hour of laps after regular practice. He knew the coach did paperwork in his office each day after the team had left, so he figured he could use the pool without any trouble. When Coach Fulton approved the plan, after making some changes, Jerry posted it on his bedroom door. It was the first thing he saw in the morning and the last thing at night.

When he arrived at the pool after classes, he usually saw Tony or Tanya — or any number of others on the team he'd gotten to know better. Some of them were really helpful. But everybody had work to do, and Jerry was no different.

One day when he thought everyone else had left for the day, he found himself doing the breaststroke in the middle of lane three with Lars on one side and Wayne on the other. The two of them had started out after him and had crept up on him as he counted out his measured number of strokes.

Jerry made believe he didn't know they were there until they were right behind him, a stroke away. He stopped suddenly, dipped beneath the water, and backpedaled for a few seconds. Then he came up behind them, swooped forward, and started splashing them with an exaggerated butterfly-type stroke he made up on the spot.

"Watch it!" shouted Lars. "Whale alert!"

"Thar she blows!" cried Wayne, splashing water in Jerry's direction.

The three of them kicked and splashed at each other until, exhausted from laughing, they crawled out of the pool. Then they laid high fives all around and Jerry knew he had two more buddies on the team.

❖　❖　❖

After a few days of practicing the basics, Jerry felt he had gained a lot on the two strokes that were newest to him, the breast and the butterfly. He didn't even feel foolish doing some of the land drills that helped to strengthen his kicking and breathing.

Once, after a really strenuous session practicing the butterfly, he said to Tanya, "You know, when I see little butterflies dipping in and out in our backyard garden, they seem so light and feathery. But that is one tough stroke! I mean, I've watched you, and you know what? You can be real fierce out there!"

"You know what?" she said, smiling. "I've watched you, too — and so can you!"

"So when's your next meet?" David asked as they waited for the school bus one morning.

"A week from Saturday," Jerry answered.

"And?" David asked.

"And what?"

"And what events are you going to be in?"

Jerry shook his head. "Too soon to tell."

David wouldn't give up. "You going to swim in the five hundred again?"

"I told you, I don't know," Jerry insisted. "Besides, what difference does it make? As long as I help out the team."

"Yeah, sure," said David. He didn't sound convinced.

"Listen, small fry," said Jerry. "You'd better watch out I don't feed you to the sharks. I meant what I said. I just want to do okay in any event I'm in. Sure, I'd like to win. But I'm still a long way behind some of the others. I'm just going to do the best I can."

Jerry saw his younger brother staring at him. This time it looked like he had gotten his message across.

Gradually, the coach let Jerry practice his crawl a little more each time.

"Your armwork is a little strange," said the coach. "But it works for you. You have the kind of stroke that holds up for the long haul. I don't think I'm going to train you for the sprints. There's a whole bunch of kids who can do that well already. Just keep up the good work at practice. How do you feel about your other strokes?"

"Pretty good," said Jerry. "The butterfly and the breaststroke seem a little easier now."

"Good," said Coach Fulton. "And the backstroke? Comfortable?"

"Sort of," Jerry said, mumbling a little.

"It's an important stroke to have down," said Coach Fulton. "Keep working on it."

So Jerry stuck to his routine. He didn't skip one moment when he was supposed to be practicing the backstroke. He was determined to master it once and for all — and to be good enough to swim that stroke competitively.

At first, he kept this to himself. But after a while he decided, Hey, I know the kids on the team well enough by now. I can talk to them about it.

So he did.

"Maybe it's because of the pause," suggested Lars. "You know, the way you have to just hold for a second at the end of a complete stroke of both arms. You don't really do that with any other stroke, so it seems funny."

"You're not afraid of sinking, are you?" asked Wayne. "Some kids have a real fear of going under on their backs."

Ace Willoughby offered this idea. "Just imagine that you're the leader of the pack and everyone wants to be able to see your ugly mug. Can't do that when you're facedown in the water."

That broke everyone in the locker room up. No really good pointers followed.

Jerry decided that he could learn a lot by keeping an eye on the best backstrokers on the team. There was no doubt that Lars and Wayne were on top of that list. Number three, he discovered from checking out the season's record, was Tony Kendrix. There was no way he'd beat out those guys. But he had to go after a spot on the backstroke roster. He had to make his mark on the toughest part of swimming for him.

Tony never said anything about all the work Jerry was doing on the backstroke. He was willing to do laps with him or to check out his drills on every stroke. Mostly, it seemed to Jerry, he liked working out on the freestyle.

"I'm not interested in the five hundred," Tony confessed. "I mean, I'd do it if the coach wanted me to. But I think I'm better on the shorter distances."

"Like the fifty freestyle?" asked Jerry.

"Uh huh," said Tony. "And one hundred and the two."

"Freestyle?"

"Right," Tony nodded. "And the backstroke. I think that's where I can really do the team some good."

Jerry didn't say anything about that. Deep down, he was glad Tony wasn't interested in the five hundred. But he hated the idea of competing with him in the backstroke. Tony had been a pal from the beginning. He might have quit swimming altogether if it hadn't been for Tanya and Tony. And now he might have to go directly up against one of them.

13 ≋≋≋

The Wednesday before the final meet of the regular season, the coach made an announcement.

"We have a two-hour practice scheduled for today," he said. "We'll all go through some drills on the four basic strokes during the first hour. Then, I want to devote the second hour to just the backstroke."

The backstroke! Has he been reading my mind? Jerry wondered.

"It's one area where a lot of you need some work," Coach Fulton went on. "But not everyone is going to be doing it during the meet. So, just the names I read off, please stay, while the rest of you can take off. Okay, for extra practice on the backstroke, I want to see the following —"

He went down the list alphabetically. Within seconds, Jerry knew that both he and Tony were among the group putting in the extra practice on the one stroke that was a real challenge for both of them. And so was Tanya. And, of course, so were Lars and Wayne.

Tony gave him the thumbs-up sign when his name was called. Jerry smiled and gave one back to his pal.

"Okay, everyone," said Coach Fulton when the second hour began. "Let's all get into the pool and form lines in the six lanes. Everyone, boys and girls. And mix it up. I don't want all of one or another."

Usually, they were kept apart. Jerry wondered what the coach was doing. They weren't going to be entered in the same events. Why mix them up?

He didn't have to wait long for an answer.

The coach moved around and switched people in different lanes. "You, over there. Paul, get behind Jillian. Tony, move into the lane on your right, in front of the group.

"You all have your own strengths and weaknesses," Coach Fulton explained. "I want you to take a good look at someone you haven't really noticed, probably, and see what you can learn from him or her. Get yourselves ready, and let me see you do fiftys at five-second intervals. And watch. Open your eyes and your minds."

Jerry couldn't believe it. He was right behind Tanya. What was he going to learn from her? He watched her all the time, and it hadn't really helped him yet, he thought.

Tanya was fourth in line. After the first three swimmers had taken their place at the end of the pool and pushed off, it was her turn.

Jerry looked at her closely. Little wisps of gold hair poked out from under her bathing cap as she stood for one moment with her back to him, facing the edge of the pool. Her arms were at her sides, her shoulders gently sloped, her head erect.

She looks really comfortable, Jerry thought. Really relaxed.

Then, she quickly positioned herself for the start and pushed off with a real spring.

Wow! She really takes off! thought Jerry. Or maybe it just seems like she does because she's so relaxed before that. I bet that's where she gets all her energy, from that little pause. After that, the rest of it is ice cream. Maybe that's what she's been doing all along — and I just never paid attention.

He tried it when it came time for him to take his turn. He couldn't let go of all tension completely, but he was a little looser for a moment before push-off. From then on, he knew that he was doing better. He felt that he had really gotten one clue that would help him master the backstroke once and for all.

When each lane had gone through two rotations, Coach Fulton blew his whistle.

"Okay, everyone out of the pool," he said. "Take seats for a second while I set up some trial races. Okay, in lane one I want —"

He went through two girls races — a fifty-yard and a one hundred — before he came to the boys. Tanya was the clear winner in her race. Jerry was pleased for her and delighted that he had found out her "secret weapon."

"Now, we'll try a hundred-yard boys backstroke."

He's not even starting with the sprint, Jerry realized. He must have that one all decided.

"Let's have Lars Morrison in lane one, Jerry Grayson in lane two, Tony Kendrix in lane three, Wayne Cabot in lane four, Paul Prescott in lane five, and

Sammy Wu in lane six. Move it, we don't have all day."

There was no time to get psyched up for the race. Jerry guessed that the coach was using this trial race to decide who would swim this event on Saturday. After all the work he'd put into it, he wanted to make the cut. Didn't he deserve some recognition for all that practice?

"Is everyone ready?"

They stood in the shallow end of the pool, all facing away from the water. "On your mark!"

That's when Jerry usually tensed up. Instead, he tried Tanya's method. He dangled his wrists in the cool water and shook off some of his nervousness. He tried to let all the pressure drain out through his fingertips, to let all the tension simply disappear.

"Get set!"

Now it was time to position himself — and he did.

"Go!"

For the first time since he started this whole swimming thing, Jerry felt comfortable doing the backstroke. He ran quickly through his list of do's and don'ts. Everything checked off.

It was amazing. He used to feel a little like an

ocean liner forging its way across the raging sea. Now, he felt more like a sleek sailboat skimming along the top of the waves with the current. His arms were great, flexible, outstretched paddles. His legs were synchronized flippers, propelling him along.

There was no problem about staying in his own lane now. Everything felt right as he approached the first turn. His outstretched fingers touched the side of the pool and he went into action. Down went his head, and over went his body in a somersault, and then came the twist back into position. A quick push-off with his feet and off he went, back down his lane.

Jerry knew from the splashing around him that he was in a race, but he paid no attention to who was on either side. And, without an announcer over the loudspeaker, there was no outside information. This was fine with him. He could concentrate on his own performance.

After the third turn, the splashing got more intense as the six swimmers poured it on. This was the final lap. It was the last chance to forge ahead and make a run for it.

Jerry drew on all his resources. His body had been well trained by now to perform the backstroke. But more than that, he was in excellent condition from practicing regularly for the last few months — and from years of sports training before that.

His arms reached farther back than he ever thought they would stretch. His legs kept up a perfectly synchronized kick from the thighs down. His speed increased until — at last — he touched the edge of the pool. The race was over.

Usually, when he'd finished doing the backstroke, Jerry felt a great sense of relief. But now it was a lot like the end of a sprint. He was exhausted and excited all at the same time.

But how did he do? Where had he placed? flashed through his mind.

"Good work, Lars," said the coach. "You, too, Jerry. You almost overtook him in that last lap. Wayne, you got off to a slow start, but you made up for it and came in third. Tony, you were close at fourth. Sammy, you were fifth. And Paul, you were right on his heels. You all did fine. Now, let me see the next group of boys."

Second! That was the best he'd ever done in the backstroke. And he'd gone up against such veteran swimmers as Wayne — and Tony.

What if the coach put him in for the hundred backstroke instead of Tony? After all, Tony'd placed fourth. Why couldn't Wayne have swum a really bad race? Or even Lars? This was exactly what he didn't want to happen.

While these thoughts were running through his mind, Tony came over to him and clapped him on the back.

"Way to go, champ!" he said. "They're going to have to refill the pool when you get through!"

"What do you mean?" asked Jerry.

"You're drying up the water with all that heat you're pouring on," said Tony. "I'd be jealous if I wasn't so proud of you. With all the work you've put in, you deserve it."

Here was Tony, possibly eliminated from the one event he wanted to do well in, congratulating him. It was as if Jerry had beaten him out for a slot in the batting order, but Tony didn't mind. After all, it was for the good of the swimming team.

For the first time, Jerry had a sense of what that really meant.

14 ≋≋≋

The first thing Jerry remembered about that Saturday morning was the sound of the "heat bug" outside his open window. Mom always said that meant it was going to be a real scorcher.

"Can we go swimming today?" asked Lucie, sloshing her soggy cereal back and forth with her spoon.

"Don't be a dummy," said David. "We're all going to the pool, but we're not going swimming. We're going to watch Jerry in the swimming meet."

"Are you going to be in that long, long race again, Jerry?" Lucie asked.

"I don't know," he said. "I'll have to see what the coach decides when I get there."

He couldn't tell her how much he wanted to swim in more than just one event. Placing in one of the top three positions in a number of races was how he could really help the team. After all, it was the final score that counted, wasn't it?

"You kids finish up," said Mr. Grayson. "Jerry, I'll run you over to the bus when it's time. Why don't you straighten out your room meanwhile?"

"I thought I'd brush Yogi," Jerry said.

"That's what I was afraid of," said Mr. Grayson, smiling at him. "That dog is going to be down to bare skin if you brush her any more!"

"A bald Yogi!" cried Lucie through a mouthful of cereal.

Jerry could hear her giggling as he went up to his room.

It wasn't that much of a mess, but it would help pass the time to clean it up.

First he picked up all his clothes that were draped over everything — his dresser knobs, desk, chair, reading lamp, bedposts, and bookcase. He stashed some of them in drawers, put some in his laundry bag, and shoved most of the remaining pile in his closet.

Curled up on her dog pillow in the corner, Yogi watched all this activity with a curious eye.

"A place for everything and everything in its

place," said Jerry. "That's what Mom always says. Well, it's all out of sight, anyhow."

He was about to close the closet door when he noticed his baseball glove on the top shelf. He reached up and ran a finger along its supple leather surface.

The one touch was enough to trigger a flood of memories. He really loved baseball. And he still planned to play in a lot of games. But who said he had to limit himself to just one sport? And who said he always had to be on the school team? Same as swimming, now that he knew more about it. As long as he gave all he had whenever he played in any sport, that's what really counted.

With that thought in mind, he finished his cleaning up and called downstairs, "Ready!"

On the bus to the meet, the coach read off the roster.

Jerry listened as Tanya's name was called out for the hundred-yard backstroke, the hundred-yard butterfly, and the two-hundred-yard freestyle relay.

"Wow, you're really gonna be doing some swimming today," Jerry whispered to her across the aisle to where she was sitting.

When Coach Fulton finished with the girls, he called out the names for the boys events.

Tony was scheduled for the fifty-yard freestyle, the hundred-yard freestyle — and the hundred-yard backstroke. The coach had decided to put him in after all — along with Lars and Wayne. So, despite Jerry's showing in that practice race on Wednesday, he still wasn't good enough at the backstroke after all.

But there was another surprise in store for him. He heard his name called out for the fifty-yard freestyle as well as the five-hundred-yard freestyle.

When Coach Fulton had finished reading the list, the bus arrived at the Weaver Middle School pool, where the meet was to be held. As they got off, the coach pulled Jerry to one side.

"You're probably wondering how I picked you for the sprint, aren't you?" he said, walking toward the locker room with the rest of the team. "I know you don't think of yourself as a sprinter, but we need some help in that race. And I think it'll give you a good chance to warm up before the five hundred. So, don't hold back, give it everything you've got."

Jerry thanked the coach and ran off to get suited up.

In the locker room, he took some good-natured ribbing from some of the other guys.

"From fifty to five hundred, you've got it all, slugger!" said Lars.

"Yeah," said Sammy Wu. "You can take a nap in between races."

There was some good advice, too.

"Watch out for the sprint," said Tony. "Even though it's just fifty yards, it's a lot longer than it sounds. So pace yourself a little so you have something left for the finish."

"Thanks, Tony," said Jerry. "And good luck in all your races. I'm glad you're in the backstroke. Some day I hope I'm good enough for that one, too."

"You're good enough," said Tony. "I think the coach just wants 'old reliables' in there during this meet. You'll get your chance sometime."

As they came out of the locker room into the pool area, Jerry got a quick adrenaline rush. It was becoming a familiar sensation.

The public address system blared out a welcome

and then went on to set the stage for the competition ahead.

"This is the last meet of the season for these two teams. The Bolton Blues bring with them a strong record of five to two, having won their last three meets with outstanding scores. The host team, the Weaver Beavers, have an identical record of five to two but have won their last four meets. So we can expect some exciting events out of these two teams."

This is where the flip-flops inside my stomach usually take over, Jerry thought. But as he stood for the singing of the national anthem, he was surprisingly calm. Maybe he didn't even have to be standing in the water for Tanya's "moment of relaxation" to work for him.

"Our first event will be the girls fifty-yard freestyle —"

"The next event will be the girls one-hundred-yard breaststroke —"

One by one, the races were run.

Tanya won first place in the hundred-yard backstroke and took second in the hundred-yard butterfly.

Lars took first place in the hundred-yard backstroke, Tony came in second, and Wayne finished third for a clean sweep by the Blues.

"The next event will be the fifty-yard boys freestyle. Swimming in lane one for the Beavers will be Jay Funchion, in lane two for the blues — Jerry Grayson . . ."

Okay, thought Jerry as he walked across the cold tile floor to the starting block. All the rest was preparation. This is now for real.

15 〰〰〰

How long had it been since he'd been swimming? One week? One month? Two? Right now, it seemed like the most natural thing in the world to him.

As Jerry stood on the block waiting for the starting gun, he felt completely relaxed. There wasn't a flip-flop in his stomach. He knew exactly what he had to do to perform well in the fifty-yard sprint. There would be two laps, with a single turn in between. There wasn't a second to waste.

And then the announcement came:

"On your mark!"

Silence fell over the pool area.

"Get set!"

His body had been hanging loose, letting all the

tension drain. Now it turned into an arc of coiled steel, ready to spring forward in an instant.

BANG!

And the race was on.

Jerry slashed his way through the water, arm over arm, legs churning up a fierce cascade of foam in his wake.

He touched the far wall of the pool and instantly flipped over in a perfect turn. The recovery set him off rocketing toward the finish line at the opposite end of the pool.

"Lane one . . . Funchion . . . Lane two . . . Grayson . . . coming down to the final strokes, and it looks like the winner by a fingertip could be — We'd better wait for the judges' decision, folks."

It didn't matter. As he stood there in the pool, unwinding from the fierce effort, Jerry could feel his heart pounding in his throat. His arms felt like rubber bands and he could hardly stand up. But nothing mattered. He knew he had done his best — and it felt great!

"It's official, the winner of the boys fifty-yard freestyle is Jerry Grayson in lane two!"

For a single second, it seemed as though the world had stopped. Inside his head, Jerry heard nothing. His eyes, too, seemed to go out of focus, and everything was blurred.

And then there was an explosion of applause. He leaped out of the pool and was immediately surrounded by the team. They wrapped a towel around him and slapped him with high fives.

Coach Fulton broke through and said, "Congratulations, Jerry. Now just take a seat and rest up for the five hundred. It'll be coming up before you know it."

He was right. The elation Jerry felt over winning the sprint had started his juices flowing. They didn't have time to settle down before the announcer was calling for the swimmers in the five hundred to take their places.

This time Jerry was joined by Ace Willoughby and Paul Prescott for the Blues. As the three of them stood there on the block, with Weaver Beavers in between, they exchanged thumbs-up signs. They knew that it didn't matter so much who won as long as the Blues carried the race.

Again, Jerry was able to let go of any tension while waiting for the signal gun to sound. At the words

"Get set!" he was as ready as he'd ever been before a 3–2 pitch. And at the sounding *BANG!* from the starter's gun, he took off like a guided missile straight ahead and into the chill green water.

This time Jerry knew much better how to pace himself. He remembered to focus on each turn as though it were the first time he was doing it. He heard noise all around him, but he completely blocked from his mind the announcer's actual words.

As he made his way back and forth, lap after lap, one thought propelled him forward — to do his best and score some points for the Blues.

The first ten laps went by so fast, he barely realized it was half over when he saw the sign at the edge of the pool. Without breaking his stroke, he glanced up and saw that it was Tanya behind the sign, giving him her biggest and brightest smile.

Stroke after stroke, he drove his body forward through the water. He felt in complete control as he turned on the throttle a little bit more after each lap now.

Fifteen.

Sixteen.

Seventeen.

Only three to go.

The roar of the crowd had increased and drowned out any possibility of hearing the announcer. Jerry had no idea who was ahead or behind and by how much. He only knew he had to keep on swimming exactly the way he knew how.

Eighteen.

Nineteen.

And then, it was the final lap. It was a race to the finish.

He pushed off from his final turn with all the spring that was left in his legs. Catching his breath and exhaling in perfect harmony with his arm movements, he began the final sprint.

Far off in the distance, he almost heard people shouting his name along with another. But it didn't matter. All he wanted to do now was reach that wall of white tile and make contact for the last time.

As he did, he could see that there was no one next to him in either lane. He had clearly beaten at least two of the Beavers. But what about the rest?

"*. . . one of the most exciting events of the day, the winner for the Bolton Blues in lane two is Paul Prescott, followed by about a fingertip in lane four,* *also for the Blues, Jerry Grayson, and in lane one, for the Weaver Beavers . . ."*

He had taken second place! He'd scored again for the team! He'd done his best, and it had paid off. Now he could really collapse on the bench and relax for the rest of the meet.

After a round of hugs and high fives and slaps from the team, he settled down to watch the next event. It was the two-hundred-yard backstroke, and Lars was favored to win by a wide margin. All season long he had piled up victories in the backstroke, and this was expected to be his crowning moment.

As the announcer called out the names, Lars walked over to the side of the pool to climb in and take his position in lane two. Just at the edge, he heard someone call out to him, "Go, Lars, go!"

Instinctively, the tall swimmer turned in the direction of the shout and, without seeing that he was so close, he tripped or slipped, and started to fall. He caught himself just before he hit the tile at the edge of the pool — or worse, toppled over into the water. But when he straightened up, Jerry could see that he was in pain.

Lars managed to get into the water and take his

position at the start of the race. But when the starting gun was fired, he couldn't push off.

The judges called for a false start. Coach Fulton rushed over and talked to Lars, who was white-faced as he floated in the shallow water.

Then the coach called for two boys to come over and help Lars out of the pool and into the locker room. The team trainer went in right after them.

Coach Fulton signaled to Tony, who had been sitting next to Jerry. Even though Tony wasn't a seasoned long-distance backstroker, he'd have to do what he could for the team.

The race got off again to a good start. But without Lars, it wasn't as exciting as everyone expected. Something was missing for the Blues, and they failed to do better than a third by Wayne. Tony came in fifth, but the coach congratulated him just the same. Jerry could hear Coach Fulton saying, "I'm proud of the effort you made, Tony."

As they waited for the announcer to call the next event, the coach told the players on the bench that Lars had sprained an ankle and that he'd be okay in a few days. But he was out of the meet for the rest of the events.

"What else is he scheduled to swim?" Jerry asked. "Isn't that it for him, anyhow?"

Tony shook his head.

"Lars is supposed to be swimming the backstroke in the two-hundred-yard medley relay. Now the coach is going to have to find a replacement."

"Why not you? Or Wayne?" Jerry asked.

"Because he doesn't want to burn us out," said Tony. "We've each been in at least four events."

And done everything they possibly could for the team, thought Jerry. They placed that goal above individual achievement. That's all they had in mind.

"Jerry," called the coach. "I want you to go in for Lars in the relay. You've never been in a relay before, but it's only two laps. And I think that sprinting is your best shot in the backstroke. Do you know how the relay works?"

Jerry was about to say, "Sure!" but he caught himself. The coach didn't go for anyone acting cocky. And besides, he only thought he knew. So, instead, he told the coach, "I think so. But could someone run through it with me?"

"Wayne! Go through the moves with Jerry over

there on the side," said the coach. "Talk him through the backstroke part of the relay."

Wayne moved over and started to tell Jerry what he had to do.

"Is your leg okay now?" Wayne asked.

"It feels great," Jerry said.

"Okay, you start off in the pool. Remember to push off with every bit of muscle you can find," said Wayne. "And don't let up after that. There's only one turn, so make it a clean one. Randy will follow you with the breaststroke and Silvio goes after him doing the butterfly. They're not all that strong on sprints, so you have to set them up real good, okay?"

"Gotcha," said Jerry. "Who's the anchor?" he asked.

"Ace," said Wayne. "He's real good doing the free-style in a medley, but he's not a great come-from-behind swimmer."

"Oh, boy," said Jerry. More pressure, he thought.

Wayne finished describing the backstroke part of the relay. Then he added, "The score's real close. This could be the deciding event of the meet. So don't screw up, slugger."

Jerry could tell that the whole team was depending on him to start things off in the right direction. It was his chance, once and for all, to do something for the team much more than for himself.

"Will the swimmers for the two-hundred-yard medley relay please take their positions!"

Jerry huddled with the other three Blues swimmers. They exchanged quick high fives before he left to get into the pool.

As he got himself into the starting position, he summoned every bit of concentration he owned. He started off with Tanya's "secret weapon," that moment of complete relaxation, just before the sounding gun went off.

BANG!

He sprang back into the water with terrific force, lashing backward with one arm after another in perfect harmony with his steady kicks.

Within seconds, he touched the opposite edge of the pool solidly and spun instantly into his turn, emerging less than a stroke behind the backstroker for the Beavers.

By sheer energy and determination, Jerry pushed himself harder than he ever had in any athletic event. When he reached the edge of the pool at the end of his second lap, he was a full stroke ahead of the competition.

That little edge inspired Randy, who ploughed his way through the breaststroke laps to maintain the lead. Silvio's butterfly lost a little on his turn, but he was neck and neck as it came time for Ace to take over.

As Jerry watched, the veteran freestyler for the Blues rocketed down the pool for the final two laps, outpacing the Beavers anchor just enough to pull ahead by a few inches.

But that was all it took. The Bolton Blues had won the medley relay — and the meet!

The team and all their fans crowded around the relay swimmers. It seemed as if everyone at the pool wanted to congratulate them on their hair-raising victory.

Coach Fulton shook Jerry's hand and gave him the thumbs-up sign. Then Lars, followed by Wayne, worked his way over to him. They hugged him and slapped high fives on him before they were swept away by their own well-wishers.

As the crowd bore down on him, Jerry found

himself getting closer and closer to the edge of the pool. In fact, he realized he was in danger of falling in.

Suddenly, Tony and Tanya broke through the crowd and pulled him clear.

"Whoa!" shouted Tanya. "We don't want to lose this guy just when we found out his big secret!"

"Oh, yeah?" said Tony, acting very serious. "What's that?"

"He's the one with the winning stroke!" said Tanya.

As they started to cheer, "Jer-ry! Jer-ry! Jer-ry!" he knew that right then he had to be the proudest kid in the world.